———— ◆ ◆ ————

I still did not know who was in the house.

The nearest telephone was in an alcove in the turn of the stairwell. I went toward it. I tried to look only toward the telephone and not down the stairs. Inevitably, however, I was impelled to look. Nothing was to be seen. Only the empty stairs leading to the small hall.

I tried the phone, but it was dead. I walked down the stairs to the door.

In one corner stood a figure, face averted, head down, quite still. I could make out the outline of the quilted, hooded gown that had been worn by my ancestor, the old astronomer.

I knew now who had come back.

TAROT'S TOWER

Jennie Melville

FAWCETT CREST • NEW YORK

TAROT'S TOWER

THIS BOOK CONTAINS THE COMPLETE TEXT OF
THE ORIGINAL HARDCOVER EDITION.

Published by Fawcett Crest Books, a unit of CBS
Publications, the Consumer Publishing Division of CBS
Inc., by arrangement with Simon and Schuster, a division
of Gulf & Western Corporation.

ISBN: 0-449-24001-0

Printed in the United States of America

10 9 8 7 6 5 4 3 2 1

One

———◆———

The day when I went back to Axwater, it was as lovely as I had remembered it. The lake a shining silver, the beech woods heavy with foliage, rich with color and dappled deep with shade. Here and there an old apple tree stood. How did they come to be there? I never knew, for surely these woods were immemorially old, part of that primeval forest that stretched across the land before Caesar and his Romans came.

I had arrived in the woods early. It is a bad habit of mine to be early, but today I wanted to be there in good time, so that I could walk slowly through the trees to see if it was as it had always been. Everything was as I remembered it. I suppose we had known it would be unchanging and this was why we had settled on it for our meeting place. Suitable for our unchanging feeling for each other was the unspoken idea, I suppose. Had our love been unchanging? Was it possible? My cynical eldest sister, Catherine, tells me that in her experience no feeling lasts longer than ten years and eight is a good average, and this had been six years, and years of absence at that.

Almost every day, until we were torn apart, Piers and I had met in the woods looking down on the lake. Forty days of complete happiness, I suppose that's not bad in any one lifetime. I suppose we thought it could go on forever.

Then on the same day I heard that I was to leave for South America to join my father, Piers had learned that he was leaving with his parents immediately for the Far East. Behind his back a family crisis had been brewing up. His father was leaving the army and going to Singapore to take up a civilian post. It was our first intimation of how vulnerable we were to a world beyond our control.

"I don't even have an address to give to you to write to," I remember saying to him.

"Nor I." Piers was white with anger. "I suppose one day they'll tell me where we're going to live, but at the moment they don't seem to know themselves."

"Why don't we just cling together? Like leeches?" I was always the most impractical. Or the more in love. I have to say that now.

"No good, my dear girl." Piers could be adult when he chose. "It wouldn't work. No, I know that I'm going to be a doctor. Somehow, somewhere, I'm going to qualify." He took my hand. "Let's make a pact. Let's meet here on this spot in six years' time. We are going to be pulled apart now by circumstances we can't either of us control. I can't even give you an address to write to. Nor can you. But let us swear to each other that we will meet here, on this spot, at this hour of the day in six years' time. Come what may, Chris, I swear and you must swear, too."

"I swear." Tears sprang hot into my eyes.

6

I did try to write once to him, sending a letter to the address where he had lived at Axwater in the hope that, somehow, it would reach him. Perhaps he tried with me also. I know I never had a reply.

Caught up in my father's life, not free, traveling constantly from place to place with him, I was helpless. I was so much younger than my sisters, Catherine, Iris and Sarah. And yet I don't blame any of them for what happened to me and Piers. It was the summer when everything fell apart: when Catherine's marriage ended, when Iris and her husband were in Australia, and when Sarah was ill and in the hospital. Thus it was a time when there was nothing stable or settled in my life at all.

And it all started so quietly: what ended in tears and blood began with love and laughter. Someone showed me a photograph the other day, one I did not know existed, a picture of Piers and me holding hands and smiling at each other. A bad photograph, it is, and one taken at a distance. Plainly we were unaware we were being photographed, but there it was, a loving moment from the past.

Now I was back.

I sat down beneath an apple tree; the tiny, sweet apples were already ripening. Old-fashioned russet apples, they were, more golden than red. Apples of the Hesperides, Piers had called them. I had forgotten his words until this minute. By the apples I knew I was standing on the right spot. There in the trunk of the gnarled old tree was the hole we had used as a letter box. Perhaps there was a letter there now. I put my hand in. No, nothing, just powdery dust and dry leaves.

I leaned against the tree and looked down the slope, through the trees to the silvery lake. A natural pool, it was irregular in shape, spiked with little inlets and gullies. There was no one in sight. The woods were empty. I was quite alone, and I sat down to wait. Expectant, hopeful.

I rarely smoke, but I had brought some cigarettes with me on purpose and I lit one now. The action marked me off from the girl who had waited here, the girl who came running, hair flying, bubbling over with excitement and happiness. Silly, young and impetuous.

I wondered if he'd changed, if I would even know him. Or, humbling thought, would he know me? But I guessed I would know him: *le coeur a ses raisons . . .*

The cigarette finished, I paced up and down. I heard the trees rustle and I swung around, but only a squirrel stared down at me curiously from his branch. A car started up and moved away on the road below. Apart from that there was silence.

It was a tranquil scene but I felt far from tranquil inside. In my pocket I had a small transistor; I sat down with my back against a tree and turned it on, very low. From somewhere a full-hearted orchestra was halfway through a piece by Richard Strauss. *Don Juan*, I think it was. Sophisticated yet romantic, the music seemed to match my mood. I suppose it was how I wanted to see myself. But even more, how I wanted Piers to see me.

The music stopped. Over quickly, I thought. I looked at my watch: twenty minutes had passed.

One bright apple fell to the ground.

"What are the apples of the Hesperides?" I had asked Piers. "Where do they come from?"

"From the happiest place in the world: the Isles of the Blessed where the Hesperides, three delicious nymphs, guard the apples, which are golden."

"Three nymphs?" I'd joked. "Sounds like my sisters. They're always looking for some golden apples." Which made my sisters sound more mercenary than they truly were. The trio have influenced my life profoundly, my

8

parents' marriage having ended before I was five years old, and my father quickly marrying again. But I was cross with them that day, they were so much older than I—Catherine twenty years my senior—and had so much power over my life, whereas I was so weak to touch theirs. Things have changed a bit since then.

Back in the present, I looked again at my watch. Now thirty minutes had passed.

I walked down to the lake and looked at the gleaming water.

He had not come. Perhaps I had never expected he would. After all, six years is a long time when it encompasses the years between sixteen and twenty-two.

I had to face the fact: I had kept our appointment, but he had not. It was a bitter little fact to swallow. I felt desolate as I walked away. Underneath, I was angry too: I had been made a fool of. I remembered our last meeting so vividly. He had held my hands tight in his and said, "We are going to be pulled apart now by circumstances we can't either of us control. I can't even give you an address to write to. Nor can you. But let us swear to each other that we will meet here, on this spot, at this hour of the day, in six years' time. Come what may, Chris, I swear, and you must swear, too."

I had sworn, tears in my eyes. I had come, and he had not.

I made my way along a narrow bridle track toward the tower of the old observatory, where I was staying. A strange place to stay, you might think, but the fact is, I was there for the rest of the summer (it was August now) and would stay into the autumn if I felt like it. Known locally as Old Noll's Finger, the observatory had been built over two centuries ago by Sir Oliver Warwick, my remote ancestor and an astronomer of his day, a pupil of Isaac Newton, and a friend of William Herschel. I suppose I

9

had inherited something of his interests, for I was now myself the newly qualified possessor of a degree in geophysics. When I went for a preliminary interview at my university and was trotting out my attainments, they said, "Mathematics is all we care about. For the rest, as long as you can read and write, that's enough for us." I remember Catherine saying in horror at this, "My dear, you won't be educated." Catherine herself, I may say, can't spell and can't add, and if she ever reads a book it's of the most frivolous sort. But somehow, yes, she is educated. She always knows the right fact at the right time and the appropriate moment at which to produce it.

In due course I stopped traveling with my father; I went to Bryn Mawr; I took a good degree. But I said no to Penn, and decided to see what a British university could do for me. Bristol, I'd heard, was good for my particular subject, which had changed from pure mathematics toward a study of this planet, earth. To my father I said that I felt déracinée and wanted to get back to England, and that, anyway, I was keen to do some work in Sir Oliver's observatory. He accepted the pull of home, but in my own mind I knew it was Piers who was pulling me back. Of course I had met other boys, and I liked them too. I wasn't precisely a nun; but every so often I would remember Piers and the intensity of his gaze as he made me promise, and inside me an obstinate little voice would say, Yes, it was real, that moment. I will hold to that.

Well, I had kept my word and it had brought me to Axwater in high summer, and to disillusion.

As I walked through the trees, delicately picking my way along the path, affecting an ease I did not feel, I heard the noise of branches cracking behind me.

I spun around. Hope rising, irrepressible, ridiculous, perhaps it was Piers. Late, but come at last.

There *was* someone there. I could see a figure through the trees.

I turned back up the slope. I saw a tall man approaching down the upper curve of the narrow path. Now I could see him; now again he was masked by the branches, thick with trailing leaves.

But there had been something in the set of his shoulders that I knew.

I started to run, I got round the curve, and there he was. "Piers," I called triumphantly. "Piers!"

I almost had my arms round him. "Oh, darling, darling," I said. "I knew you'd come." The words were out before the disappointment hit me like a blow and winded me. I didn't speak. I stood there, like a fool, wordless.

This man was not Piers. True, there had been something about him that, just for a moment, reminded me of Piers. But this man was older, and fairer, both taller and thinner.

He looked at me without recognition. "What was that you said?"

I got my breath back. "Nothing."

"You said something." There was just a trace of irritation in his voice.

"It was a mistake."

He raised his eyebrows. He had an expressive face, and I have seldom seen skepticism more clearly expressed.

"I mistook you for someone else," I said.

He looked at me as if he disliked what he saw.

"I'm sorry," I said. "It was quite an accident. A mistake." I turned round to go back the way I had come. I was still too sick with disappointment to take much notice of his reaction. Then I heard him say, almost to himself, "I hope it was."

I swung back. "What do you mean?"

11

"Unless someone put you up to it?" Tone and face were definitely hostile now.

I swung round, stung into speech. "No. Of course not. Who would do that? I told you. It was a mistake." I swallowed, my throat felt constricted so that the words were hard to say. "Just for a minute, no more, I thought you were someone I knew. Someone I expected to see. That was all. And I'm sorry."

He gave me a very strange long look at that. For whatever reason, I had somehow confirmed his worst fears. "Really?" was all he said, skepticism once again to the fore. "Who are you? I've never seen you before. You're not a local girl. I suppose you wouldn't be."

"I don't know what you mean by that. I don't know what you mean by any of this talk. For what it's worth, I am a local girl of sorts. My name is Christabel Warwick. I'm spending the summer at the observatory."

"Oh, you're *that* girl."

"Yes, I'm that girl. And I'm sorry I spoke to you. As I said, it was a mistake. Stupid of me. Good day." Once again I turned away, but a word from him stopped me.

"I'm sorry. I shouldn't have said what I did. I'm afraid I am a little . . ." and he hesitated.

Paranoiac, I finished silently to myself. But he didn't look mad. A little fine-drawn perhaps, a bit somber, as if he didn't find much joy in his life, but not crazy.

"A little too hasty," he finished. He gave me a kind of bow and whistled, as I imagined, for his dog. He looked the sort of man who would have a lurcher or a red setter at his heel, but to my surprise a tiny, bright-eyed, button-faced creature appeared through the undergrowth, tongue lolling out of its mouth. Behind it came another even smaller, and then another. Three sleeve Pekingese. They took no notice of me at all, but fixed their eyes passionately on his face. I thought I liked his dogs better than him.

I didn't wait for any more; I wanted this encounter over and went back down the path. I had passed round the edge of the lake and was moving up the slight eminence on which the observatory stood, when I remembered that he had not told me his name.

He knew who I was, but of his identity I had not the least idea.

By its very nature there are a lot of stairs up to the tower. You had to be sound in wind and limb just to live there. I had my living quarters on the second floor, where Sir Oliver himself had lived. Iris's husband had put in a small kitchen and bathroom of the most exquisite and modern sort, which no doubt would have delighted Sir Oliver if the old scientist had ever been able to see it. He had been a man of the future in his own time.

I rushed up two flights of narrow stairs and arrived in my living room. "Catherine?" I called. "Are you there?" My sister had driven down from London with me, meaning to claim—though without ever saying a word about it—her quarter-share of the property. Catherine has a great sense of property, for all she's so generous.

It's a rather tricky business furnishing an observatory but Iris's husband, or his interior decorator, had solved it well. My floor was covered with a pale and very thick carpet, like rough grass, into which the feet sank luxuriously: I usually threw my shoes off and padded round in stockinged feet. On top of this any normal furniture would have looked wrong and so the decorator had dispensed with it, and had strewn the floor with great, gentle, sacklike objects covered in the softest Spanish leather, into which one sank as into a pillow. He had provided a low table of pale, unpolished marble and then, to liven things up, had stuck a red Chinese cabinet, the same age as the observatory, against one wall. We were lucky that Iris's husband was so rich. And so loving.

But for anything practical like writing a letter, or eating, one was obliged to use the kitchen. I could hear Catherine whistling as I went in, and then a great tide of soapy water slapped over my feet.

Catherine has a gentle, pretty face, and of all my sisters she is the most like my father, who appears to be just a successful, extroverted businessman but is very sharp and canny inside. He saw the resemblance himself: "She's not too scrupulous, your sister," he said to me one day. "And she's more than a shade ruthless." He always called her "your sister" when he was at odds with her, as if he withdrew from parenthood a degree. All the same, he loved her best of all his children, as I loved her best of my sisters. I even loved her *because* I knew she would cheat if she had to.

Catherine was whistling as she scrubbed the kitchen floor. She delighted in physical activity of any sort in a way I can't say I do myself.

"You're not supposed to scrub that floor," I said. "The tiles are specially sealed so that all it requires is a mopover. It shouldn't even need that very often." The floor was covered with a pretty mosaic of blue and white tiles, every one of which was now rich with lathered soap and running with water. It looked like a Roman bath on cleaning day.

Catherine rose from her knees cheerfully. "Never mind, it did me good to scrub them. What about you? Had a nice walk?"

"Lovely," I said. Without another word I got down to mopping up the excess water. There was always a good deal of tidying up to do after Catherine. She watched me

14

without interest, as if she were in no way responsible for all the lather.

"Hope you have a happy summer here," she said. "Not the nicest place in the world to stay alone, I shouldn't think. But you say you like it."

"I do. What have you got against it?"

"Bit oppressive, isn't it? Not that I believe in Sir Oliver's ghost, of course. Who could? But upstairs in the big chamber almost open to the skies . . . I don't know, you feel the influence of the heavens, don't you? It's almost as if the stars were bearing down on you."

"I don't feel like that. When I was little I used to worry that I might fall off the edge of the world into the blackness—it is black, you know, it only appears blue to us here because of our atmosphere—but now I like to look at the stars."

"Well, everyone to their taste," said Catherine briskly. "And mine is for a nice window-shop down Sloane Street on a spring morning. Hopeless, aren't I? But I could substitute the Rue St. Honoré or Madison Avenue, if you preferred. Or that nice little street at the back of the Via Veneto. I've always fancied it. Does the old boy's telescope really work still?"

"Oh yes, all attended to and in working order. I got a grant from a learned society to have it put right. It's a very simple instrument. But all the same, I've had someone come down and show me how to manage it. The man who repaired it, in fact. After all, my skill is only amateur. It's supposed to be *this* planet I know about and not the rest of the solar system, although one picks up a bit."

Catherine looked at me admiringly. "I do love the way you talk . . . as if the universe was your parish. Still, I suppose I deserved it for that bit about the little street off the Via Veneto." She picked up her coat. "Well, I must be off."

I grinned, feeling better for my contact with her. "Stay till it's dark," I said, "and let me show you the night sky and the stars."

"I ought to drive back—" But she was curious, and I could see she wanted to stay. "Where do you sleep?" she said. "I can't see anywhere."

"I drag two of the big leather pillows together and lie on that. They are beautifully comfortable," I said. "It's what the architect meant. I've seen the plans: this part is called the 'living-sleeping-loving area.' Only I haven't got a lover."

We had supper and waited for darkness to come. The observatory was very quiet at night; even the trees that stood around it seemed to have the quality of silence. The building was on the crest of the hill, raising its head through the trees, so that when you were on the top floor and the great window had been drawn back on its ancient system of ropes and pulleys you seemed to be floating above a sea of leaves. I loved that feeling and cherished it silently, not wanting to express it to Catherine, for fear of destroying it.

The night happened to be calm and clear, so that the stars stood out boldly.

"No moon," observed Catherine.

"Not yet. It will rise later." I was adjusting the simple controls of the telescope. My ancestor, obviously anxious to observe in comfort, had erected a kind of wooden cradle under the eyepiece. Here, semi-recumbent, he could survey the skies.

I helped Catherine get into the right position. "Here you are. This is a Herschelian telescope, as you might expect. The very latest model when Sir Oliver built it. He made it himself, you know, with the help of a Dutch optician."

"What's all that mean?" asked Catherine, settling herself comfortably.

"Oh, only that you are looking through an eyepiece directed obliquely at a mirror which is reflecting the image projected by the lenses. It wastes less light than the Gregorian instrument."

"It's quite small, isn't it?"

"The lenses are twelve inches—yes, that is tiny, although it was big for its period. About ten years later than this, Sir William Herschel built one with a lens of forty-eight inches. I think he must have influenced what Sir Oliver was doing, perhaps even helped him in the building of this device, as it has so many of the features he later built into his own instrument. We know the two men were friends."

"How?" asked Catherine, always more interested in personalities than objects.

"Oh, letters and so on. Herschel was the up-and-coming young man when Sir Oliver was old, just as he himself had been young when Newton was old."

"Do we own the letters?" Ownership, too, interested Catherine.

"No, they are in a museum." I made another adjustment. "Now look. Lie back, relax and look."

"Like being at the dentist," giggled Catherine, but presently the majesty of what she saw overcame her and she fell silent.

"How little it makes one feel," she said at last. "Do people always say that?"

"Very often, I think."

She took another look. "So many of them," I heard her murmur.

"Oh yes, millions of stars in our galaxy alone, and beyond that, countless numbers of galaxies. Hard to comprehend, isn't it?"

Catherine slid out from under the telescope. "I'm afraid he must have been a much thinner person than I, old Sir Oliver, but then he didn't have a bosom, and he certainly can't have had hips." She's lavishly built, is Catherine, always on a diet and perpetually falling off it. She gave herself a little shake like a dog, setting herself to rights. "Now I must be off to the only star I'm really interested in."

Catherine designed, and had made up in her own small workroom, the most delicious and original clothes. In her heart she designed them for herself, so that to wear them you had to be tall with a certain sort of beauty. Thus she would never be rich or succeed in the mass market, but for those women with the right sort of look she was unsurpassed. Increasingly she was including men as well as women among her clients, making for them robes and jackets of quiet magnificence such as a Manchu prince or a Florentine duke might have worn. Her "star" was a pop singer called Peterborough. It was only just in time. Last year Catherine had come very close to bankruptcy. Now the crisis seemed over. By his passion for his clothes, and hers, Peterborough was enriching her.

"Keeping you busy, is he?"

"Yes, bless him," said Catherine fondly. As she got into her car and prepared to drive off, she went back to a point that had evidently interested her. "Funny, isn't it, how the color and brightness of the stars vary when you look at them through a telescope? With the naked eye one doesn't notice so much, but tonight I was struck by how they varied."

"It depends, partly, on how close they are."

She started the car. "Glad to see you looking better now. When you came in from your walk I thought you might be going to be ill."

18

"Nothing the matter with me at all," I said, a slight tremor in my voice.

"Let me know if either this place or the summer gets too much for you and I'll come running."

"I will." I waited for her to drive away.

"Oh, by the way, I didn't know you knew anyone down here."

"I don't."

"Well, I almost forgot to tell you, but someone rang while you were out—a young man, nice voice."

"Who was it?" I said quickly. Too quickly probably, for she gave me a perceptive look.

"Don't know. Rang off without telling. But he said he'd ring again, so you'll find out." She put her foot on the accelerator. "Funny thing, he called you Chris. Haven't heard you called that for years. Not since you were about fifteen or sixteen."

"That's it," I said steadily. "Since I was sixteen."

She waved her hand cheerfully and the car sailed off. She had seemed happy enough, but I thought she was uneasy. Catherine had something on her mind. I could always tell with her because her eyes seemed to change color, to bleach from blue to gray. They had been very gray today.

I went and sat on the steps leading up to the open door of the observatory. Light from inside flooded out. Sir Oliver had built himself this three-story tower of local red brick when he was a spry old man of sixty, and had lived there for another twenty years, a contented hermit, studying the heavens, his solitude occasionally assuaged, so legend said, by the attentions of the odd country girl, which wasn't bad at eighty. I've seen the pale, oyster-colored silk suit with fur-lined hood that he wore for his cold night watches of the stars, and he must have been a seductive old gentleman, my ancestor. Tiny and neat,

19

judging by the size of the suit, into which I could not begin to cram myself. Of course, I know that successive generations have gotten taller and heavier, but even so, I think Sir Oliver must have been small-boned and slender.

With the passage of the years the difference between astronomy and astrology—not always precisely defined in seventeenth-century science, in any case—had become blurred, and an aura of magic hung over the observatory. The local girls went there to study the signs of the zodiac painted on the ceiling, to make out their futures and to giggle. It was believed that if you looked at the new moon through the curved glass of the roof window it brought you luck, and that to go at midnight to pick the gilly flowers that grew around the base of the tower and to sleep with them under your pillow brought you happiness in love and fertility in marriage. What with one thing and another, my distinguished ancestor lingered in folk memory more as a Merlin figure than as the pragmatic scientist he had been in fact. Sir Oliver was really interested in observing the laws of nature, but he had gone down in history as a master of the black arts. No wonder his ghost was reputed to walk. I never saw him, nor ever expect to, being a rationalist myself.

Piers had called me Chris. For years now everyone else had called me Christabel. Surely it had been Piers who had telephoned me.

It began to feel cold and I got up and went inside, up the sixty-three steps to my viewing room. Half of me was still deeply concentrated on Piers, but I forced myself to think of other things. There was one subject which still gripped me.

The telescope was still in place, turning its eye on the night sky. I slipped into the viewing position and began to gaze. Some people say that the summer is the worst time for star-gazing, but I think it has a beauty of its own.

Yes, there was the Pole Star. There was the Plough in the north and still fairly high up. I could see Cassiopeia, and Arcturus. Now there was Capella, low in the north. The brightness of Vega led me to the constellation of Scorpio, and from this my eye traveled eastward to Sagittarius, the Archer. Then beyond lay three large, dim constellations: Hercules, the Hero; Ophiuchus, the Serpent-bearer, and Serpens with whom Ophiuchus is struggling. Back to Scorpio my eye traveled for a moment, and then westward to find Libra, the Balance.

I paused for a while and let the peace and majesty of it sweep over me. Impossible to see all this and dwell too much on one's own affairs.

Beyond Scorpio, in the region of the sky which would be filled in autumn by the constellation Pegasus, not visible now, was a bright star. A clear golden object. I let my eyes rest on it with pleasure. Surely it was bigger than yesterday?

I hadn't drawn Catherine's attention to it, and since she never read any part of a newspaper except the fashion page, she had not read about it, nor did she know enough to find its appearance in any way remarkable. And yet it was so. At the moment it was probably the most remarkable object up there. To look at it was one of my purposes in returning to the tower. A wanderer in space, a stranger, was arriving. A great comet was moving into our skies.

In my excited and emotional state I felt I had to talk to somebody. Amateur astronomers, like radio hams, always have a contact with whom they keep in touch, telephoning to pass on sightings and astronomical gossip and speculation. Mine was called Hector and lived over a hundred miles north. He was always at home at night, always awake. I had never met him; our friendship was conducted entirely by letter or the telephone. I always imagined him as an elderly bachelor, as he seemed to have no ties and nothing to distract him from his observations, but for all I knew he could be much married with ten children. I rang him now.

"I've seen it," I said. "It's beautiful, isn't it?"

He responded at once. "Yes, it's coming along fine, just fine. What a spectacle it will be in a month or so. Right over your head, I reckon. It'll be hanging in the sky like a Chinese lantern. Did you notice the tails?"

He had a stronger instrument than my antique. "I haven't been able to get much detail yet," I said.

"Three or four at the least, streaming 'way behind, and two shorter ones closer in. What a sight," he said with enthusiasm. "I wonder when it was last here before?"

"Great" comets cannot be predicted because their periods run into thousands or even millions of years. It seemed to me an omen that the arrival of this wanderer from space should coincide with my reunion with Piers.

"If it doesn't disappear," went on Hector briskly. Pessimism was his vice.

"Oh, surely it couldn't?"

"Comets aren't nicknamed the ghosts of space for nothing. They have been known to disappear." He added, "Not everything arrives that is expected."

I put the receiver down. A delicate, subtle emotion, compounded of disappointment and apprehension, flooded through me at the horrid appositeness of his comment. My summer of the ghosts, I thought. Oh, it mustn't be, it couldn't be! Surely Piers would come.

I stayed in the next day to wait for another telephone call. A quiet day, with sadness creeping in on me all the time like a slowly rising tide. I wasn't exactly idle—there

22

was so much to do—but all the time I kept myself busy, I was wondering why the telephone didn't ring again. And when I wasn't wondering about this, I was asking myself why Piers had chosen this way to get in touch with me again. I tried to be sensible, but there were as many reasons as there were ways of asking the question. He might be ill; he might have been prevented from traveling to Axwater. After all, the call could have been coming from anywhere, anywhere in the world. Catherine hadn't said it was a local call. She might not have known. Or cared.

But then I had to ask myself, How did he know where I was? To this question too there could be an easy answer. I was using the shops in the small town near at hand. Somehow, somewhere there could be a contact. A person who knew us both and who had said to Piers, "Oh yes, Christabel Warwick, I've heard she's at the old observatory by Axwater."

Yes, you could rationalize everything away and I did. Surely the call must come soon?

But still the telephone did not ring, and as the day wore on I gradually became convinced, in a sad, sour kind of way, that it would not ring while I waited for it. So eventually I took the receiver off the hook (how terrible if it should ring while I was not there) and went out.

Although Axwater gave the impression of extreme isolation, in fact there was a footpath which skirted the fields and came out by the church, around which clustered a few houses. This was the hamlet of Steeple Minden. From this point a bus ran several times a day into the nearest small town, Brayford.

Today I took this path. There were various supplies I needed from Brayford. Anyway, I like local buses and the people you meet on them. But I had another motive, hardly expressed to myself but of which I was quite conscious.

I was going to revisit the places where Piers and I had

been happy together. Unconsciously, without wanting to admit it, I was looking for Piers. Ever since he had failed to come to our meeting place I had been conscious of an emptiness inside me. I had thought about him for so long, held his image in my heart so tenaciously, that now I felt hollow. It was a dead kind of misery, almost worse than pain. Where are you, Piers? Why didn't you come? were the questions that kept pounding and pounding around in my mind.

I walked slowly down the path, taking my time, and emerged by the stile that led into the churchyard. I climbed over it and walked on the path that led through the tombstones and graves and past the church. The church had been built in the late sixteenth century in the pretty red brick one saw so much of around here. The graves that were dotted about the grass looked as old as the church, although in one far corner of the churchyard, under a great yew, there was a cluster of newer tombs. The clock in the church tower struck the hour as I passed, four strokes in a gentle, mellow old voice. At the same moment a bus approached from the opposite direction.

It stopped to let me get on, and with me an elderly woman who had come hurrying out of a house across the road. I paid my fare and settled myself comfortably in the seat by the window just behind where the driver sat. He was in no way shut off from the rest of the bus, although his seat had a higher back with a little box hooked on where he kept the tickets, so he was able to keep up a running conversation with the passengers.

"See you came out of the doctor's, Miss May," he said to the woman who had got on when I did. "Nothing wrong, I hope?"

"No, I was just taking him a pot of my strawberry jam," she said, "and he gave me some of his honey." She

24

had a neat, precise way of talking, as if speech mattered to her, and as if she were one whose words would be listened to.

"Ah, I remember those bees, Miss May," said the driver in a tone of reminiscence. "Proper bad stings they gave me once."

"Well-deserved stings, John Weaver," she said. "You'd no business to be poking around the hives."

"Ah, it was after that lesson you gave us on bees, Miss May," answered the driver. "Natural history, it was, and not honey that interested me."

So then I knew who Miss May was, or what she had been: the village schoolteacher.

"Know where you're going, miss?" called the driver to me. Of course he had me marked down as a stranger. Miss May didn't say anything, but she looked at me with calm interest.

"Yes," I said dreamily. "The Aviary in the park and the Creamery Coffee Shop."

"Been there before then, have you?"

"Yes, years ago."

They had been meeting places for me and Piers; I wanted to see them again. I suppose you could call it a sentimental journey.

Perhaps I had other hopes also, strong inside me but unexpressed. The hope that I would walk inside and see Piers sitting there, the hope that someone would say, "Oh yes, he was here earlier today, talking about you." Silly, childish fancies, I know, but who in love has not known such hopes?

Miss May leaned forward. "Both are still there," she informed me in her precise voice.

Miss May had one other precise observation to make to me: "It's a good day to see birds," she announced, nodding her head. Later, I was to find she meant exactly what she said.

The old attendant at the Aviary had been a man who took one's money and watched suspiciously all the time one studied the birds. The new attendant was a woman, and a young one at that. She didn't seem at all suspicious, nor even very interested in me. She took my money and went back to a magazine she was reading. I could see the title upside down. *THE STARS AND YOUR LIFE*, it read. Well, so what? I thought. Who knows what influence the stars have after all?

The little building had been given a clean coat of paint and the inside walls whitewashed, thus wiping out the graffiti I seemed to remember being there, but a fresh generation of wall scribblers was already building up its record. We had not added to the collection, regarding ourselves as beyond such tricks.

The flocks of little birds looked exactly as I remembered them. The smaller birds, the canaries and budgerigars, fluttered around with the bright-eyed aimlessness of their kind. Round the corner, where a few gloomy-faced parrots huddled on imitation tree branches made of plastic wood—which they obviously knew and despised—I looked in vain for someone I remembered. There had been a mynah bird called Joey in this corner. Joey had gone, his place occupied by a tribe of brightly colored flutterers unrecognized by me.

I walked back to the girl sitting studying her stars. "What's happened to Joey?" I asked.

She looked up. "Joey?" she said vaguely. "I don't know. Is he a friend of yours?"

"He's a bird. Or he was. A mynah bird. Everyone called him Joey."

She put down her magazine. "I'll ask Dad." She called over her shoulder, and from an inner sanctum appeared

26

the identical old attendant I remembered from the past, ready as ever to give me his suspicious stare. "Dad, this lady wants to know what happened to Joey."

"Dead," he said.

"I supposed it must be that," I said, sadly. After all, what could happen to birds but death? They didn't retire or go away for a change of air.

"Died two years ago. You remember him, do you?"

I nodded. "One summer, six years ago, I used to come regularly. I'm sorry he's gone."

"Ah, he was a wicked natured old bird. Took a nip at you as soon as look at you. I wasn't sorry to see him go." He was looking into my face. "Came in regular, did you? I always used to say I knew the regulars."

"You wouldn't remember me, of course." I was turning away. "Anyway, six years ago I looked different."

"No, I don't know your face." He gave me an assessing stare.

"It was the summer of the great storm, when lightning hit your roof, and all the birds huddled in one corner, frightened." I hadn't recalled that episode myself until that very moment. Now I remembered the storm and the curtain of rain that had fallen dramatically from the sky, bursting apart with lightning and rippling with thunder. Piers and I had been happy prisoners in there with the birds for over an hour.

"I remember now. Wait a minute. Are you the kid that used to come in with the tall boy?"

I nodded, wordlessly.

"You helped me clear up after the storm. Never saw you again after that."

"I went away."

"Saw *him*, though."

"Did you?" I was surprised. It had never occurred to me that Piers would have visited the Aviary without me.

27

"Yes. Came back. All by himself. All one afternoon he walked up and down in here. I came in and looked. Didn't know what to think."

A vivid picture sprang into my mind of Piers coming back to where we had met, pacing up and down and thinking about me. I hadn't known. How could I have known? But it seemed a terrible loss now, not to have known.

"And know what he was doing? Had to tell him off sharp." He wagged a finger at me. "Cutting his initials in the wall, he was. 'Big lad, like you,' I said, 'ought to be ashamed of yourself.' C. W., he'd got there, large as life."

Not his initials but mine. Mine. "Which wall?" I asked.

"The wall opposite where old Joey used to be. 'Course it's all gone now since we redecorated."

"So I suppose." I tried to smile.

He rocked backward and forward on his heels. His gaze was inward now and thoughtful, not suspicious. "There was something else about him: I saw his picture in the papers not so long ago. Least I thought it was him. Sure of it. Can't remember what it was, though. Either he did something or he *was* something . . ." He fell silent.

I waited.

"No, it's gone. Can't remember. Memory's funny, isn't it? Can't put my finger on it."

Leaving him still muttering to himself, I went to look at the wall. Behind me the bright birds fluttered, swooping back and forth from perch to perch.

It was true that a thick coat of whitewash had gone over this wall, but the afternoon sunlight was making the shadows deep. I could see the faint indentation where Piers had carved. The ghosts of my initials, C. W., were still there, faint and shadowy underneath the effacing whiteness. I put out my hand and touched.

28

Piers had suddenly come back very close to me. I felt I had only to reach to take his hand.

My fellow traveler on the bus had been right: it was a good day to visit the birds.

I found my way to the Creamery Coffee Shop by memory. It wasn't very far from the Aviary. Looking back, it was clear that Piers and I hadn't been walkers and that the long strolls I had thought I remembered had existed more in my imagination than in fact. Of course, we had always been talking. I'm sure my memory didn't let me down there, we had talked all the time, there was so much to say. Had we listened to each other at all? I had an uneasy feeling that Piers might have had things to say to me that I was too communicative to hear. He was older than I; his character had been more formed. Aware of changes and developments in myself, I thought I might have a surprise or two in store for him. I'd grown up, grown harder and tougher, not quite the gentle, dreamy little creature I had been, although I knew she still lingered there underneath, ready to let me down if I wasn't careful. But Piers, in spite of his greater sophistication, inevitably would have changed also. Probably he would have some surprises for me too. We might not even like each other.

Now that I thought about it, could I blame him for not keeping our appointment yesterday? For delaying it? Was it not possible he was even now quietly observing me? I gave a hasty look over my shoulder, as if I might catch him at it if I looked quickly enough. No one there, of course. The street was almost empty.

But if he had been there, if he was watching me, could I blame him for that either? Hadn't curiosity been one of my motives for turning up in the woods?

I got to the Creamery Coffee Shop before I expected.

All the distances seemed to have shrunk somehow. I am told this always happens and that places seen again after a long absence are always shabbier and smaller than their remembered image. This part of it didn't come true with the Creamery. While I had been away it had bought up the next two shops and had expanded and grown glossier and smarter. The old Creamery had been shabby and quiet. The new Creamery was bright and full of color and had got itself a long counter with stools where it sold something it called American ice cream. I looked at it in surprise. The old Creamery had never heard of ice cream, and gave the impression of having barely heard of America.

I wandered in, full of doubt, and sat on a tall stool. I ordered a peppermint and chocolate ice cream, and to my great surprise the man who ladled it out and handed it to me in a slender glass was the same man who had poured out the coffee when Piers and I had gone there.

I ate my ice cream very slowly, and then, to spin things out, ordered some coffee. When it arrived it tasted of cardboard, but then so had the coffee of the old Creamery: in this respect life had not changed. In fact, the more I looked around me, the more clearly I could see that the old Creamery was there underneath and that the ice-cream parlor and the gleaming tiles and the bright paint had just been fixed on top, like a piece of stage machinery.

The place was almost empty, but a group of youngsters were sitting at a table in the window, giggling and talking together. They looked very young. One of the boys came across to the counter where I was sitting. "Another coffee, please, Tommy." He took a look at what Tommy was pouring. "Black, please."

"Why didn't you say so before?" demanded Tommy.

"It's the only sort that's got any taste, Tommy." The

boy gave me a grin, accepted the black coffee with a brisk "Thank you, Tommy," and went back to his friends.

Tommy's gaze met mine. He smiled.

"You've changed the place since I last came in," I said.

"One thing leads to another," he said. "Started with some new blue and white paint with matching tiles in the kitchen and ended up with me serving ice cream." He spoke with great good humor, as if he liked it all. "We get a nice crowd in here," he said.

"It's six years since I was here," I said happily. I *was* happy. Irrationally convinced that I was very close to Piers, and that our reunion would be a triumphant success. I shifted my position slightly so that I could keep an eye on the door. He might walk through it—throwing it open in that decided way I remembered, and then standing on the threshold for a moment, looking round to see if I was there. I always had been.

"Six years? Oh well, you'd expect changes. I was here, though."

"I know," I said.

"Got a good memory, have you?"

"Well," I temporized. I didn't want to explain how vivid were my memories of this place—how I could even remember the scuff marks on the old floor, now replaced with gleaming plastic marble. "Well, I liked it here. I used to come with a friend." Already I was saying more than I had meant. But, of course, I *wanted* to talk about it really. *Needed* to, you could say.

"Happy memories?" he said with a smile.

I nodded. "Yes." I know I smiled, I couldn't stop myself.

He read a lot into that smile. "You look a bit young to be talking about memories, though. The future it ought to be, at your age." He was giving the final polish to a row of ice-cream glasses as he spoke.

"Well, I have hopes for that too. I used to come in here with a boy called Piers Temple—"

He stopped polishing his glasses and put the cloth down on the counter.

"Of course, you wouldn't remember, not me, not him, but I remember you."

He took up the cloth again and rubbed very hard at one particular glass. "I remember him all right."

"Do you? Do you really?"

"Yes. Came in here a lot last summer. Got to talking with each other. He told me his name."

"Oh." I was a bit nonplussed. So Piers had been back in Brayford, perhaps even back to Axwater, very recently. It was unexpected news. Silly to let it throw me, though.

"He was visiting his uncle, got a place hereabouts."

Again I was surprised. "I didn't know he had an uncle living near Brayford."

"Bought a place. Ramshackle old house. No one else wanted it. Turned it into a restaurant. Then he closed it. Didn't pay, I suppose." He shook his head. "Certainly prospered for a time, though. Of course it was expensive, but there was plenty willing to pay and visit the animals he kept on the grounds. The Rolls and Mercedes you'd see driving up there—not near the poverty line, his customers. I suppose he lost interest. Don't know what happened to the animals. Lovely little things, they were. Small, old-fashioned breeds he went in for—White Park cattle and the barking deer. I daresay they're still roaming."

I nodded. It explained how Piers could have known of my arrival, and helped to explain his telephone call. He was really quite close to me all the time. The idea gave me a strange feeling, half exhilaration, half apprehension. It was strange he hadn't turned up in the woods. I supposed that to have done so might have seemed

32

childish behavior to him. I did not think he would have forgotten.

"What's the address?" I asked. "What's the house called?"

"Folly House, near Axwater," he said slowly.

I knew the house. It was an old house on the other side of Minden Ridge, the hill that faced the observatory across the lake. Sir Oliver had built a house there for himself while he worked in the observatory. As far as I knew, the ownership of the two properties had been separated shortly after his death.

"I suppose I could go and visit Piers there," I said dreamily.

"What's that?" Tommy said.

I smiled, willing now to reveal my secret. "We had an agreement, Piers and I, made, oh, years ago, to meet in the wood above Axwater. Yesterday. I went, but he didn't turn up. Wretch," I said fondly.

Tommy turned his head away and picked up another glass. He applied himself to giving it a very good shine. Then he said, "No, he wouldn't be there. He couldn't be. I'm sorry you don't know. I can see you don't. He's dead."

Two

—————•◆•—————

A wasp had got into the Creamery and was buzzing round and round. I could both hear it and feel it. I put my hand up. A wave of dizziness swept over me.

"Are you all right?"

I closed my eyes, then opened them again to find Tommy's face staring anxiously into mine. "Are you all right?" he repeated.

"No, no, I'm not all right."

I put my head down on my hands and closed my eyes. As if from a distance I could hear Tommy's voice. He was saying something, but words had temporarily lost their meaning for me.

I felt him put a hand on my shoulder; he must have come round to my side of the counter. I forced myself to open my eyes and raise my head. Tommy was staring down at me with an anxious expression on his face.

"You've gone very white. It's all my fault: I ought not

to have spoken out the way I did. I could kick myself." He was very upset. "Are you going to faint?"

"Oh no. I'm better now." It wasn't quite true, but I was steadier.

"You don't look it."

"It was a shock, that was all." I heard my own voice speaking and to my surprise it sounded calm, but it was a lying voice to be so calm. A light had gone out in my world and everything around me was smaller and darker and meaner than it had been before.

"I could see you didn't know about him being killed; I couldn't let you go on talking about him as if he was alive when he wasn't." Tommy was distressed, his large brown eyes eloquent.

I was still walking in the dark but I had to comfort him. "No, indeed you couldn't. I'm glad you told me."

"No, you're not: you couldn't be. But I had to speak."

The buzzing had stopped. I was able to think more clearly. "There was something you said—that he was *killed?*"

"Yes, he was killed by a car that didn't stop. They found his body on the roadside and his cycle by him—all smashed up. It was all in the papers, inquest and all."

"When?" I could just bring myself to utter that one word.

"A year ago. In late summer—there were blackberries in the hedges. It rained that day after a long dry spell and I remember thinking, Ah, that's the end of summer. The rain fixed it in my memory."

For a year, while I had still thought of him as alive, Piers had been dead. Dead for a whole year, dead, while I dreamed and hoped, dead while I waited in the woods for him to come.

"It was a tragedy," said Tommy soberly. "He was such

35

a nice lad. What a waste, what a waste. Going to be a doctor, too. Think of all the good he could have done." He shook his head. "Life's very unfair."

"How did it happen? Who was the motorist?"

"Never found out. Nasty business." Tommy seemed to put the words together reluctantly. "If he'd been discovered earlier he might have been saved. Died from shock as much as anything."

There was a note in his voice that made me question. "What do you mean?"

"People said—that is, I *heard* it said—" He stopped. "It was a nasty business." He stopped short again.

"Go on, I want to hear."

We were interrupted by a burst of laughter from the table in the window. A boy and a girl came over to Tommy. "Ice cream, please, Tommy."

Tommy leaned over to me. "Look, I can't talk now. Come back later tonight. There's hardly anyone here by eight o'clock. I don't know why we stay open."

I nodded. "I'll be back." I slid down from my stool. Behind me I could hear voices cheerfully demanding strawberry ice cream.

"Wait a minute," said Tommy. "I can't let you go without telling you I know who you are; you're the girl who's Christabel. He used to talk about you."

"I'm glad."

"Oh, he did, he did. Mind you, he was upset about what you did."

"What I did? But I didn't do anything."

There was another call for ice cream, which he had to heed. "Yes, coming," he called. To me he said, "He didn't say much . . . just somehow you'd let him down."

"But I didn't, I didn't," I choked.

"Look, like I said, I can't talk now. Tonight? Right."

36

I went outside and wandered through the streets of the little town, desolate and without comfort. I wondered where I could go. I knew the hour had to be lived through. I couldn't escape, it was a door I had to walk through to whatever lay on the other side. The present pain must be endured until it changed into something else. My mind said that, given time, it would do this, but my body could only register the present chill and sickness which, like the symptoms of an illness, attended upon my grief. It might be a mortal illness. I could not be sure, but I had youth and strength on my side and, no doubt, I would recover.

Eventually I found myself sitting slumped on a seat in the little park where the birds lived. Without my knowing it my feet had taken me there.

The golden light of a summer evening still filled the sky, but up there in its own darkness the great comet was coming closer and closer. I never quite forgot about it.

"How could it be like this?" I said aloud. "How *could* it be?"

My cry was more than a protest against blind fate, it was also a genuine question. Instinctively I knew there was much more to know about Piers's death.

I looked at my watch. Time had passed. In a short while I would be seeing Tommy. From him I would learn more.

There was something I wanted to know about the end of the world, and I thought I would try to find out in the public library in Brayford. It wanted about twenty minutes to eight o'clock, and I thought I might just have time. All amateur astronomers with a taste for history (and most of us have, for a sense of the past is necessary for study of the stars) know that in the old Anglo-Saxon

Chronicle for the year 900 there is an account of a comet "like a lion with tails and ruff" which dominated the heavens for some weeks, an omen which excited and terrified the populace. The chronicler records that many people thought it hailed the end of the world, an event they were always, in any case, on the lookout for. I wanted to see if I could find this entry, which I had only heard about and never read for myself, and see if perhaps this could be our comet, the great comet, now approaching. Would it arouse alarm this time it came? Comets are often greeted with superstitious awe. Perhaps no one this time would regard it as heralding the end of the world, but my world had certainly taken a shock.

My experience of libraries in little towns like Brayford is that they very often have a surprisingly good section of reference books and history books.

The librarian was young and enthusiastic. She received my request with no more than a blink. "We close at eight, but I shall be around for some time after that. I think you will find what you want in the Rolls Series. Volumes twenty-two and twenty-three. The second volume contains the translation. Unless you read Anglo-Saxon?"

I shook my head silently.

"Are you a student?"

I saw her looking at me, and knew she was taking in my dress, which was, of course, made by Catherine. It was narrow and striped, thus making me look like an elegant giraffe. Can a giraffe look elegant? In Catherine's world he could.

"A graduate," I said. "Is it all right for me to read here?"

"Oh yes. I'd better get your name and address." She pushed a printed form across to me. "Just a formality. But then you can always come in as you want."

I filled it in: Christabel Warwick, The Observatory, Axwater.

She was reading it upside down as I wrote, a useful skill for anyone and especially a librarian. "Oh, that's who you are. How interesting that you are trying to set it all in order. Can you really *live* there?"

"Easily."

Diffidently, she said, "I'm so interested to meet you. I am the secretary to a small discussion group. I wonder if our group could see round the observatory some evening? Meet there, perhaps? Some of our members are *very* interested in the stars."

I made the sort of noise which can mean either doubt or assent. She took it for assent.

"We have a very lively set of members, ranging from a beauty expert to a Himalayan climber: he told us about Tibet."

"I may not be here so long," I said, "but I'll try and arrange something. Where did you say the Anglo-Saxon Chronicle was?"

"Bottom shelf, book case on the lefthand side of the window. In there," and she nodded through a pair of swing doors. "Opposite the files of newspapers," she called.

A tide of familiar warmth and quietness swept over me as I went through, and I knew that one of the reasons I had come was to seek support from the sort of surroundings I was used to, away from the world in which people one loved died violently and so unexpectedly.

But that this was an illusion, and that no comfort was to be extracted from retreat, was revealed to me in the stark words of the old chronicler. "The great star, six tailed and bearing a ruff of light about its head, so that it was called the Lion Star, travelled across the heavens for eighty days and eighty nights, being visible, for the most

39

part of that time, by day as well as by night. It was a most fearful portent. The peasants in the fields at their labours would not raise their heads to look at it, for fear they might grow blind, the beasts sickened, and the animals of the chase fled and no bird sang from the trees. In summer there was great drought and the earth was like iron. Many said it portended the end of the world. True it is that many people perished whether by famine or by sickness."

I put the book down. No escape there. I had come right back to a hard and terrible world. But at least I had ascertained that the Lion Star did seem remarkably like our comet.

"Goodbye," I said to the librarian, "and thank you."

"*You* weren't long." She sounded surprised.

"No. See you soon." I threw the words over my shoulder and hurried off to the Creamery Coffee Shop. I meant nothing at all by those words, but as so often happens, they came true.

Tommy was on the lookout for me when I got back to the Creamery. I saw that he had laid out a place for me on the counter, giving me a little paper-lace mat and on it placing a pretty well polished cup and saucer into which he carefully poured some coffee.

"That's the old china we used six years ago," he said, giving me a solicitous look. "Haven't got much of it left. Nicer to drink out of than these plastic mugs. Thought you'd like it."

"Oh, I do." I tried to smile. "The coffee's good, too."

"Made it myself," he said. "I'll have a cup with you. I could do with it. So could you, by the look of you. How did you fill in the time? I know you didn't go back to Axwater. I saw the bus go back and you weren't on it. How *will* you get back?"

"I don't know," I said vaguely. "Walk."

"Five miles and no moon. Give you a lift on my motor-bike if you like. Think you could ride pillion?"

"Tommy," I said gently, "tell me what you've got to tell me and let me know. Don't worry about how I get home. I can take a taxi if I have to. Just tell me."

"Yes, I will then. You're quite right, there's no point in not being straight. I don't think it was an accident the way he was killed. Not a proper accident. He was run down on purpose."

The wasp that I had beaten out of my head earlier was back there now, buzzing about louder than ever.

"But that would be murder," I gasped.

"Yes, I think it was."

"But why do you say this? How *can* you? How do you know?"

"My cousin is a policeman. He was the first person to see the body. Other than the milkman who found him. It was early morning, see. My cousin said it didn't look right. Not the way the body was lying, nor the position of the bike. Contrived, he called it. And his Inspector, when he came, felt the same."

"Feeling isn't enough," I said.

"He said that when the rider is hit by a moving vehicle like a van or a car the body is thrown and falls in a certain way, hands, arms and legs awry like a doll's. The bike may be some way off, or dead close, even on top. But your friend's body looked laid out, straight almost. And his bike was *beside* him. It's not usual in these hit-and-drive-away cases. Drive on fast is what usually happens, and no hands on the victim. The driver doesn't linger. This one did. Made it different."

"What was Piers doing down here?"

"I don't know. No one knew that either. He wasn't staying down here, and his uncle wasn't expecting him."

"I'd forgotten his uncle."

41

"Well, don't. We don't down here. He identified him . . ." His voice trailed away.

"No," I said, feeling ill; I suddenly saw the implications of his silence. "Don't go on. I suppose he was terribly knocked about."

"Yes. Face, hands, chest, that was where the car hit him. If it *was* a straight car accident. Crushed. But he had things in his pocket with his name on. And then his clothes, they were his. But my idea is that some of these injuries could have been done *after* he was unconscious or dead, to hide the way he was killed."

I sat there, seeing not the walls of the Creamery Coffee Shop, but instead that bloody, broken figure on the grass verge by the hedgerow. "What road was it?" I said.

Tommy said reluctantly, "The road out toward Steeple Minden. Where it curves round the slope of the hill by Axwater."

So Piers had died near the observatory. There was something terrible to me about that fact.

"Yes, I came on that road today. I wish it hadn't been there."

"It's a bad bit of road. The curve is deceptive. More than one bad accident there."

"So another one there *was* plausible."

"Oh yes."

"And there never was a real examination—" I swallowed "—of Piers's body?"

"Well, only what old Doctor Hadows did. From what I heard, it was a pretty superficial routine one. He wasn't looking for anything much." He leaned forward, talking confidentially: "You see, the county has no resident pathologist for forensic things—they have to use a London man if they want one. And that costs money, and money is short. So they don't call him in unless someone pushes. And old Doc Hadows was convinced it was a case of hit-

42

and-run. There were enough broken bones to make it that." He shook his head. "There was blood on the road, yes, but also blood coagulated with splinters of bone on the bike. Supposing it was run at him afterward, like?"

"And other injuries could have been covered up? He could have been stabbed or beaten to death or even strangled?" I thought that he had nothing really, no hard facts, only police gossip. Yet I found myself believing him.

"I was in love with Piers," I said aloud, but not to Tommy. I felt more as if I was addressing the wide audience of the world. It was in no sense a confidence to him. "At least I think I was. I hadn't seen him for six years but his image was still there at the back of my mind. I never forgot. I suppose that's love? Anyway, I'm never going to have a chance to find out." Distantly the world audience seemed to make some sort of response, which I must have heard, because I went on: "But that's not what's important. It's the *waste*, the waste of the life Piers could have had with someone, if not me, the waste of the life he could have had with himself, the waste of the generations that would have come after him." The audience of the world retreated and I was conscious of Tommy's face, staring at me, flushed and concerned.

"Don't cry," said Tommy.

I wiped away the tears. "Take no notice. It's not sorrow, it's more anger than anything else."

"Six years is a long time," said Tommy thoughtfully. "He might have changed. You must have done."

"Yes, if we'd met we might not have liked each other. And he thought already I'd let him down. I know all that. But at least we could have found out. Now we never can."

"He didn't say in so many words that you'd let him down," said Tommy, as if he'd been thinking it out. "He

43

said that he'd asked too much from you and he couldn't blame you."

"I wish he hadn't said that," I cried. "Because whatever he meant, it wasn't fair."

"No, it wasn't. But he couldn't know he'd never meet you face to face."

"Oh, we can't go round and round it and over and over it," I said, pushing my cup away from me. "It's done." I felt like sweeping everything away like the cup. "I don't suppose he was really killed on purpose, either. You must be wrong there. Someone ran him down and then panicked when they saw what had happened. Whoever it was dragged his body to the roadside and left it there. A terrible thing, but not murder. Don't you see?"

Tommy didn't answer, but stayed silent, staring down into his half-drunk cup of coffee, now rapidly chilling.

"Unless you know something you're not telling me," I said. I looked at his face. "Yes, that's it. You do."

"There's been a lot of talk," said Tommy. "Some of it unwise, no doubt." He stopped.

"Go on," I said. "You must go on."

"Rumor, that's all. But he died at a handy time for someone, that's all."

"What do you mean?"

"Look, I don't think I can say any more. But I can tell you who to go and see. And you won't have to go far, he's camping out by Axwater. Piers had a friend, Simon Dean. Go and talk to him."

Tommy offered me a lift on his motorbike once again and once again I refused. "I can take a cab."

He looked at the clock. "If you hurry you can catch the bus from the Market Cross. That will drop you at the crossroads just above Axwater and you can walk."

I got down from my stool. "How much do I owe you for the coffee?"

"Nothing. On me. I took it out in other ways."

I held out my hand. "Goodbye, and thanks."

He wiped his hand on a towel and shook mine carefully. "Goodbye, and look after yourself."

"Oh, I will," I said. "I always do."

I got off the bus and walked down the hill that led to Steeple Minden. There was still a lot of light in the sky and I could see quite well. Even with the naked eye I could make out Vega and Polaris. A low belt of hazy cloud masked, but did not hide, Scorpio and Sagittarius. Another couple of people had got off the bus at the same time, a young girl and a boy, and for a while I could hear them murmuring and laughing behind me, like the ghosts of Piers and me. Then they turned off into a side lane and I was alone.

The road turned and I was in the village. I could see the church and the path by the churchyard which I had to take to get back. An owl hooted from the great yew tree by the lych-gate as I went through.

All the tombstones on this side of the churchyard were ancient, the earth around them long undisturbed. I could make out the names on some of those nearest me. *Amelia Fletcher, beloved wife of Thomas Fletcher, died April 23, 1827, aged 42 years,* I read. Next door lay another Fletcher: Amelia's grandson Edward, who had died in 1907. Beyond them lay Turveys and Grazebrooks, generations of them, all testifying to the continuity of village life.

Even as I looked at them, I knew what I was going to do. In the light of the slowly rising moon I was going to cross the churchyard to look at the new tombstones.

I knew what I would find, and knew without anyone to tell me that it was this cold gray marble, the inscription undimmed by the passage of years and the stone as yet unweathered. *Piers Temple, died August 13, 1975, aged 22 years.* And underneath, in smaller letters, it said, *This*

45

stone was placed here in his memory by his uncle, Christopher Temple.

I dropped to my knees before it. "Oh, Piers," I said. "Oh, Piers."

I didn't feel close to Piers now, but far, far away, and from this arose my sharpest pain. This smooth piece of stone with its clearly chiseled inscription seemed to have nothing to do with the Piers I had known, and therefore could not connect me with him. He was closer to me by far in the woods among the trees and by the lake at Axwater.

It was only afterward, back at the observatory as I was making myself some coffee in preparation for what I knew would be a sleepless night, that I thought it was strange that Piers's uncle should erect the memorial to him. Was there no one closer to him to do it?

I didn't want to sleep. I did not want to part company with this day on which, for me, if for no one else, Piers had died. While I kept awake, he was not quite gone.

I was very conscious of the woods all around me, haunted for me by the figure of Piers. The woods had always been empty—which was, I suppose, why Piers and I had been drawn to them. In my memory we were always alone, although I knew that in fact we had been together in many crowded places, and that Piers had had one small friend, a chubby child we called Little Billy, who sometimes dogged our footsteps, following us with his big, dark eyes. No one else seemed to walk in the woods now but me and my ghost. Although I had once or twice caught fleeting glimpses of a shabby, bowed figure working here, whom I took to be a woodsman.

I changed into trousers and shirt, and then took my coffee to drink under the stars. The night was so clear that the nearest stars seemed close and brilliant, while the more distant were bright dagger-points. Some of

46

them, like Sirius in the constellation of the Big Dog, and Betelgueuse in Orion, I looked at as old friends. The Milky Way stretched in a wide white band across the sky. Hard to comprehend the immense distances and the great suns it held within that airy band.

I drank the coffee, but food was quite out of the question, the shock and emotions of the day were still churning around inside, now cold like ice, now hot like fire. It struck me that a drink of brandy would be the thing, and provident Catherine had left me a bottle. I went back into the observatory, hunted around for it, and discovered that my kind sister had also left me a little cellar of wine, some hocks and clarets, together with the bottle of brandy and one of gin . . . all her own favorites. There was even a bottle of champagne, which I didn't see myself drinking.

I poured some brandy into what remained of the coffee and drank it down. After a little while the rigors eased. I slumped down onto one of the leather cushions which gave sensuously under me. The leather was still so new I could smell it, and the fragrance mingled pleasantly with the scents on the night air blown through the windows. All around me were the sounds of the old building settling down for the night, the aged timbers contracting and little spatters of dry dust falling behind the paneled walls. I fancy there was the quiet noise of mice too. No doubt generations of mice had reared their families in the numerous nooks and crevices of the old building. Somehow I imagined my ancestor Sir Oliver had been friendly to all the animal creation and had not discouraged his household mice. I had only to put out my hand to the oak paneling to touch the carving of a small rabbit or bird or shrew. I wondered what he had done with his life outside of his science—whom he had loved, whom mourned, and by whom been outlived. I believed he had been a vigorous man in many ways, with his full share of earthly tastes. As well as little animals, the carving in the panels portrayed one or two round-cheeked, full-breasted country girls, full of invitation. The paneling was all rustic stuff, as if my ancestor had employed a journeyman woodcarver who had learned his trade on church screens and choir stalls, so full of sly humor was his work.

I got up and followed the winding stairs into the tower where the telescope was housed. Here too there was paneling, but the carvings were different. Here were no animals but the signs of the zodiac: the Bull, the Twins, the Lion and all the rest, all twelve were somewhere, if you looked.

But there were other carvings as well, which did not seem to fit into the procession of the zodiac. I had noticed a crowned woman, a chariot wheel and a man in a fool's cap, followed by a dog. Nor was this all. My eye fell on other carvings, one of which looked like a man carrying a branch of a tree, or it might have been a lamp. The wood had suffered some damage; here and there the carving had been broken away.

The lighting in this lower room was efficient but cheerless, my brother-in-law's interior decorator having thought of this as strictly a work place. Every time I had used the lighting I was surprised to see how history fled at the touch of the switch as the room filled with a hard white light from a glaring lamp. I noticed, however, that the decorator had provided two spots, angled to throw a light on the walls, which would reflect it back. Thinking that these would offer a much softer light, I moved across the room to switch them on. Decorating a panel nearby I saw two more carved figures, one male, one female, naked, holding hands.

There was only one name they could bear, I thought, and I gave it to them at once: The Lovers.

I switched off the bright light and in the reflected light this lower chamber again looked elegant. I enjoyed it for a moment, then let darkness claim the room and slid into the seat beneath the telescope.

I turned my gaze toward the area of the sky where the great comet moved into view. Even since last night it had increased in size and luster. I gazed for some minutes. Then I let my eyes turn toward deeper distances, where galaxies clustered in the constellation of Coma Berenices. Usually I found the immensity and silence calming, but tonight it was no good. Tonight nothing could stop me from thinking about Piers.

When I did sleep it was to confused dreams in which Piers still lived, in a world where comets, many-tailed, flared across the skies.

I was dragged from my sleep by a remembrance. In the early morning, when the dawn chorus of birds was just beginning, I came awake with a sentence fully formed in my mind: You had a telephone call from someone who called you Chris. Who had made that call?

With that thought I came fully awake and knew that I might as well get up. I padded over to the telephone and tested if it was in place. It remained silent. Only Catherine would have been wondering about me, and I knew that even if she had tried to telephone me and failed to get through, she wouldn't be worrying. She had unlimited faith in my capacity to look after myself. Iris only telephoned when she was unhappy, and Sarah between lovers.

I felt brisk and energetic, and since I still had plenty to do upstairs examining the boxes of papers and books—left untouched, if not since Sir Oliver's time, at least for about fifty years—I took my breakfast tray up and started to work. I hadn't forgotten what I was going to do today—find Simon Dean and talk to him about Piers.

The thought was there in my mind all the time, but I was awaiting the moment.

The history of the old observatory was a curious one. Upon Sir Oliver's death the property was inherited by his son, by whom it was bequeathed to a married daughter. All this time it had remained uninhabited and unused, dust settling on all Sir Oliver's fine instruments. About then the house where Sir Oliver had lived had been sold, separately, and had been rebuilt, becoming Folly House.

In the middle of the nineteenth century an attempt was made to tidy it up, and a caretaker was appointed, who kept the key and showed the building to such visitors as were interested. Not many came. Eventually the land was sold to a farmer, who padlocked the door of the observatory and then ignored it. Half-forgotten buildings often take on a strange life of their own, and I believe it must have been during this time that a lot of the legends grew up around Sir Oliver's observatory.

A year ago Iris's husband bought it back for the family, restored it, and presented it as a gift to his wife and her three sisters. Of us all, I think I was the only one who was pleased and I, of course, had reasons of my own.

My first quick glances inside the boxes and locked cabinets had shown me that not all the relics contained in them had belonged to Sir Oliver Warwick. Later generations had added more than their share. Indeed, I should say that a good deal of the material dated from the nineteenth century tidying-up period, when an attempt to create a good effect must have been made. An orrery and a matching globe seemed to be obviously Victorian. There seemed to be nothing of great value and nothing really very old, which somewhat surprised me. But I hoped to find some genuine souvenirs of Sir Oliver in the assortment.

Among other things was an oddly shaped object made

of lead, and my fingers explored it curiously. It was small enough to hold in my hand, but heavy. As I examined it I saw that it had rudimentary legs and a kind of knob on the top that could have stood for a head. Perhaps it was a figure of some sort, much weathered by the years.

Even this brief look through made me hot and dusty. I was glad to stop; I washed the dust from my hands and walked slowly down the winding stairs and out of the observatory into the sparkling sunlight.

It was already hot—particularly, unusually hot—as if the comet, obliterated for the moment by the sun but still there in the sky, were changing the weather.

"Talk to Simon Dean" had been Tommy's suggestion to me, implying that he could tell me more about Piers's death. Another implication of Tommy's advice had been that I would have no great difficulty in discovering where Simon was. That remained to be seen.

I walked down the slope through the short, broad avenue of poplars which led from the steps of the observatory toward the lake. It made a fine formal approach. In an old county history I had seen an engraving of the observatory showing this view at night with the moon rising. It looked eerie. Today hardly a leaf moved in the hot, still air. Axwater glittered in the bright sunlight.

Someone was swimming in the lake. I could see arms flashing in a quick crawl. It was clearly a man. A young one, I judged from the rough impetuosity of the movement. The lake was vibrating around him.

I saw he had left his towel on the grass at the edge of the lake immediately ahead of me.

The swimmer, head down, oblivious of onlookers, came toward me with quick strokes. Then he stood up, gave himself a shake like a large dog, so that the water fell from his gleaming skin, and strode toward the edge of the lake. He had a beautiful body. I had every opportunity of judging, as he was completely naked.

Then he turned his head and saw me. Our eyes met; there was no embarrassment between us. Silently I handed him the towel. I was turning away when he said, "Chris! It's Christabel."

I turned round and stared. He had the towel draped about him like a toga, but he didn't succeed in looking like a Roman senator. As far as I knew I had never seen him before in my life. "Yes, I'm Christabel Warwick," I said.

"You don't know me, but I recognized you at once. You haven't changed much. I was a friend of Piers." He gave me a look; I could see he was wondering if I knew.

"I know he's dead," I said. There was an awkward pause, only broken when I said, "I believe I could guess your name."

"I'm Simon Dean." He gave a harassed glance behind him and his gaze focused on a thicket of trees and bushes. "My clothes are over there. Give me a minute."

He hurried off, with more dignity than might have been expected. I sat down on the grass and waited. Soon he was back, wearing jeans and a white shirt, and rubbing his hair dry.

"Sorry about all that."

"No, I'm very glad to meet you." I did not add that I had been looking for him.

He was staring into my face. "It's amazing how you've remained the same. Grown up and all that, of course, but I knew you at once. I know you don't know me. But I often used to see you with Piers. I watched you. From a distance, of course." He grinned. "I admired you. But I knew I could never cut Piers out. Anyway, he was my friend. School and all that. But I know all about you."

"You mean Piers talked about me?" I was surprised at

52

that news. Somehow I had always had the idea that Piers hadn't talked about me much.

"No. Well, yes, a bit. But not in any way you would mind," he added hastily. "He loved you, you see, and he couldn't keep it all to himself. Although he tried. But we'd known each other all our lives, you see. Why, he was the first person I ever had a fight with and I was the first kid he ever bashed back. That was the way it went." He grinned again. "He could always beat me. Right down the line."

"He was very clever," I said.

"Yes, he was. You don't have to tell me. If anyone knew, I did. But he was more than that . . . well, who knows if you don't."

"Yes," I said. I let my eyes rest on Axwater. "I met Piers here, one summer. How did you know him?"

He frowned. "Do you know, I can't remember when I first met Piers. He was always there. I know we both went to the same school in the village. Nursery school. I suppose I was four and he was about the same. He could read, though, and I couldn't. Miss May—that was the schoolteacher's name—used to rub that in. Later on I could spell better, so that put me level. After that he went off with his family. They were always on the move, never settled. But for two years, just before that summer when you and he—" he nodded "—that summer, well, for the two years previous he'd gone to my public school, and we were back together again. After that we didn't meet again till university . . . it didn't make any difference, we always took up just where we left off. As if there was no difference. Piers had that quality." He looked at me shyly. "You would have found it the same."

Hesitating a little, strangely shy, I said, "You know that we had promised each other to meet here? We were sort of pledged . . . to meet in the woods."

He looked away. "Yes, I did know. Not exactly when, but I knew it must be soon. I suppose I was thinking about it. When I heard about the girl at the observatory I knew it must be you. I tried to telephone. Silly really. What could I say? Everything about you was very real to Piers."

"It was real to me, too," I said swiftly.

"I mean it went on being real to Piers. Surprising, really," he said thoughtfully. "That's what upset him, of course."

"You mean when he thought I'd let him down," I said with deliberation.

"Yes, I did mean that." Simon looked embarrassed. "How did you know?"

I ignored the question. "What exactly did he think I'd done?"

Simon shrugged. "Got another feller, I suppose. Someone told him you'd gone to America and were never coming back. He'd put two and two together, I suppose, and make out the sum."

"It wasn't true."

Simon looked at me hard, then looked away. "No one would blame you, you know. Piers never did. After all . . ." He didn't finish what he had begun.

"But it wasn't true. Can't you hear me saying it? It simply wasn't true." Exasperated, I added, "Look at me, I'm here, aren't I? Not in America."

"There's a lot of malice around," said Simon simply. "As I ought to know. Someone didn't like you, I suppose. Or didn't like Piers."

"Or did like him too much," I said. "Was it a girl who passed on the lie to him?"

"He never said who told him."

"But he believed it." I couldn't keep the bitterness out of my voice. "He might have trusted me to keep my word to him and meet him here. All right, we might not have liked each other so much when we met again, but at least I meant to turn up."

"For what my opinion's worth," said Simon, "I believe he would have come, too." He added, "If he could have."

Our eyes met. In his I could see sympathy and sadness. "Now I shall never know," I said.

"You know what happened? How he died? You did know?"

"I've been told. Something," I said jerkily, finding it difficult to get the words out.

"Not much to tell, really." Clearly he didn't want to go on with the subject. He threw a stone into the water and watched it splash.

"I believe there is. I've been told you are the person to ask."

"What?" He jerked round to look at me.

"I was told you knew something about how Piers died."

There was a long pause, during which I saw Simon's brows draw together in a frown. He no longer looked so boyish, but cold, and angry, and older.

"Who told you that?" he asked.

"Oh, an old acquaintance. He works in a place called the Creamery Coffee Shop in Brayford. He told me there was a suspicion that Piers did not die by accident, but was killed. Murdered."

"And he sent you to me?"

"Yes. He said you were Piers's friend."

Simon picked up another stone and threw it. It skimmed the water, then sank, leaving the echo of its movement behind to disturb the surface. "I tried to telephone you the other day. I'd heard you were at the old observatory. I wanted to talk to you. I suppose I've said too much already. There is also a law of slander. Not that

I think *he's* likely to take me up for it." He gave a laugh. "No, he's too canny for that."

"Who is?" I asked. "Who is this 'he'?"

"Where does murder usually come from? Ask any policeman. Look at the statistics. It's a family crime and Piers had hardly any family left, his parents were both dead. They both died in an accident, too. Ask the man who was with them when they died. Ask the only one left in the family. If you can get him to talk to you, that is. Ask Piers's uncle, Kit Temple."

"Are you telling me that Piers was deliberately run down by his uncle and left to die?" I said. "That his uncle killed him in cold blood?"

"My God, I think he did," said Simon.

We sat and looked at each other for a moment. "Why? You must have a good reason for saying that."

"Yes, I do." But instead of going on, he sat staring into the water of the lake, as if he were seeing something there. Finally he took a deep breath and went on: "All circumstantial, of course. I didn't *see* him kill Piers. No one did. As far as I know there were no witnesses. No, there were two things. First of all, something Piers said."

"Please go on," I said. "Did Piers say something to you?"

He shook his head. "No." Simon swallowed as if he found speech difficult. "He was talking to someone else. On the telephone. And he said—I heard him say—'You hate me, you've always hated me, you'll kill me if you can. You're a coward.' Then I heard him say, 'You'll kill me in a sort of accident if you can, that's your way.'" Simon's face was flushed, and his voice was thick. "You're the first person I've actually told that conversation to," he said. "Actually repeated it word for word."

"Are you sure it was spoken to his uncle?"

"Yes, I'm quite sure," said Simon. "He was on the telephone to his uncle. We were both staying with Miss May. She invited us to spend the weekend. She used to teach us when we were little kids in her school. She's retired now. Retired from teaching, anyway," he added, as if she hadn't retired from anything else. "We were sitting together in her living room and Piers suddenly said he'd got a telephone call to make. He'd had a letter from his uncle that day that upset him, I can swear to that, and so can Miss May. It came at breakfast and he went quite white as he read it. Piers always went white with emotion."

"Yes, that's true," I said.

"It's all true. Besides, there's more. Oh, it's all circumstantial again, but there's the change in Kit Temple himself. Since Piers died he's turned in on himself, he acts like a man with a load of guilt on his shoulders. Ask anyone. They call him 'The Hermit' around here."

"I see," I said thoughtfully. I wasn't quite sure what to make of all this, although I could see that Simon believed it.

"And then he sold his car after Piers died. He's never driven again." Simon's voice shook.

"The police would have checked all that, surely?" I said.

"I don't know if they looked. Or if they suspected Kit Temple. I didn't hear about the car sale myself until Piers had been dead six months. It was also six months before I saw Kit Temple again. Now it's all built up in my mind. But it's come gradually. I didn't think of it all at once."

"I can understand that," I said.

"Of course you can. Anyone could. Piers was my friend. Perhaps I have talked about it a bit too much. Not to everyone, mind. But if your friend in the Creamery knows, other people must. Like Kit Temple."

"It's puzzling," I said. "This story you've built up, it

57

doesn't quite hang together. In a way, yes, in a way, no. You don't *know* it was his uncle Piers spoke to on the telephone. Why should he kill his nephew? And why in this particularly brutal way?"

"I don't know," said Simon. "But I would swear he did."

"I'd like to meet Kit Temple," I said. "I'd like to make up my own mind."

"And what would you do then? If you decided he was guilty?"

"I don't know. Kill him myself, perhaps."

"Don't be stupid," said Simon, his voice harsh. "He'd probably kill you first."

"He might try to do that," I agreed. "But then, it hasn't happened yet," I reminded him. "So far we haven't met. This is all in the future."

"Some things you can see coming," said Simon.

"Oh, go on."

"The future is just the past with hobnailed boots on," said Simon. "Nearly always nastier than you think. And it's coming steadily toward you, and you can't stop it. But if you can read it, you're that much better equipped to face it."

"I see." I had no idea what he was talking about. "But that's not so easy to do."

"Oh, there are things you can do that help. Techniques you can use. All societies evolve them. In Tibet they've a wheel of fortune. Seems to work for some people. Just tricks, I suspect, to open the mind to things it knows anyway. Wheels, crystal balls, cards, that sort of thing." He turned and gave me a radiant smile. "Of course they don't tell everything. For instance, I might know you were coming, feel absolutely sure, but I might not know how beautiful you would be when you came."

"Of course, you must be the Tibetan expert I heard

about in the county library in Brayford. A Himalayan climber and a student of Tibet, that describes you, doesn't it?"

"I've been on one Himalayan expedition. But don't overrate me, I'm not a great climber. I shan't see the top of Everest. It's the places I like, not the struggle to get there, and that's the wrong way round. Tibet, of course, I've only studied from the outside. One can no longer get in there. It always was difficult, but now it's impossible. Forbidden territory. But I have hopes." He spoke with optimism, but I put him down as a dreamer. I wasn't sure yet if he was a dreamer who made his visions come true. He was by no means an easy character to assess, being clumsy and adept by turns.

He got up. "Come along and see my camp. I'm experimenting with various bits of equipment in preparation for my next climb. I hope to go out next year if I can raise the money." He held out his hand. "Come on. Up."

I scrambled to my feet. "Can't you see in your crystal ball?" I asked.

"Oh, I never said I used a crystal ball," he said, striding ahead. "Do you really mean to seek out Kit Temple?" he asked over his shoulder.

I caught him up. "Isn't that already revealed to you in your picture of the future?" We were near his tents now, three arranged in a neat triangle.

He stopped. "Yes," he said. "Yes, it is. I believe you will."

We were standing there looking at each other, eyes level, when we were interrupted by a voice.

"Hallo." A vigorous, cheerful figure, wearing a red cloak and carrying a basket, was walking toward us. She looked like an elderly Red Riding Hood; I recognized the woman I had seen on the bus to Brayford. "Hallo," she called again. "There you are, Simon. What a solemn look.

Been bathing, I see." She gave him a sharp up-and-down look. "Hair's wet. Dry it, please."

"Yes, I will, Miss May," said Simon obediently. "This is Christabel Warwick."

"So it is, so it is," said Miss May cheerfully. "Well, so you've come at last."

"Yes," I said, a little puzzled. So had I been expected?

"Saw you on the bus. Better go and dry your hair, Simon, my dear. I've brought you some eggs and some bread."

So she *was* a kind of Red Riding Hood, I thought, bringing food to a most unlikely wolf in the woods.

"Yes, I'm going, Miss May. Thank you for the eggs," said Simon, disappearing into a tent. "Put them in the kitchen."

"Nice little set-up he's got here, hasn't he?" said Miss May, looking round. Simon had a kind of encampment of three tents, each of which was clearly used for a different purpose. They were sophisticated modern tents, one a bright orange-yellow, another a jungle green, and the third a pale, pretty blue. "He calls that one the kitchen." She pointed to the blue one and gave one of her rich laughs. She seemed to find the idea funny. "You mustn't mind me ordering him around, you know. I've known him nearly all his life."

"I don't mind," I said. "It's nothing to me."

"Isn't it?" she said absently, as if she knew better. "Still, you can never tell. I taught Piers, too."

"I know. Simon has told me."

"Yes." She shook her head. "Funny old world, isn't it? Here's Piers gone and Simon left. I was very fond of both boys. It was a terrible thing that happened." There was a question in her voice, which I answered.

"I want to find out more about it."

"I don't see why you shouldn't," she said thoughtfully.

"Excuse me a minute." She went over to the "kitchen" and emptied her basket of the food. I couldn't help seeing that it contained a pie in a dish and a bowl of fruit as well as the eggs and the bread. Then she came back and stood beside me. "Come and see me this evening," she said.

I nodded. "I will."

"Come to supper. Bring Simon and come yourself."

She picked up her basket, wound her cloak round her, and strode off. I watched her go.

Simon, when he reappeared, looking neat and well-brushed, accepted the disposition of his evening without resentment. "I thought she'd ask," he said. "I knew she'd want to have a look at you. She's been thinking about you a lot."

"Has she?" I said, surprised.

"Yes, of course. She loved Piers. She used to bully me, but she loved him. Want to stay and have lunch? I expect she's left enough for two. She would."

I shook my head. "No, thank you. I think I must get back."

I said goodbye to him and he promised to call for me to take me to Steeple Minden. I walked back through the wood to the observatory, waving to Simon, who stood watching me from his encampment, just before I passed out of sight. I think he was still watching me.

The old observatory received me with peace and quiet. I felt very tired, a desire to sleep crept over me. I sank down on one of the soft leather sacks and closed my eyes.

Miss May dwelled in a small, neat house in the main street of Steeple Minden. She lived next door to the village store and round the corner from the doctor, and she was but a stone's throw from the church. In other words, she was strategically placed to see all and know all. There was no longer a village school in Steeple Minden:

it had been closed six years ago. The pupils now traveled by bus to a school in Brayford. Miss May was philosophical. "We must move with the times. No sense in trying to go on being an ancient Roman, when one would be better off joining the barbarians." I noticed there was often an acid flick in her remarks which belied her jolly laugh.

She poured me some sherry in a fine old glass. "Have a drink. Doctor Montague will be looking in soon. A great friend. He gave me the sherry. You'll find it's good. What's it like living in the observatory?"

"I like it." I sipped the sherry, which was indeed good, well up to Catherine's standard.

My hostess drank a good long draft of sherry herself. "I'm very interested in the old place. I hear you're tidying it up. But you mustn't spoil it."

"I won't do that." Nor, I thought, had my brother-in-law's decorator. He had been an artist who had awakened the building from its Victorian sleep and revived it.

"No, I think you won't. You seem sympathetic. An astronomer yourself, then?"

I drank some more sherry. "Only an amateur one. I started by being interested in mathematics, then geophysics. Now I play at astronomy. I'll have to get a job at the end of the summer."

"And astrology?"

"Interpreting the future through the stars? No, I don't know anything about that art."

"And yet the two sciences—I prefer to call both sciences—started together."

"In the Middle Ages," I said. "They separated a long way back. Sir Oliver Warwick distinguished sharply between the two when he built the observatory." Even as I said the words, I remembered the signs of the zodiac carved on the paneled walls of his tower. Perhaps he retained them as decoration, I thought.

62

"During the days of its dereliction, before your brother-in-law did it up, it was something of a center in the neighborhood. Did you know that? The village girls used to go there at the new moon and wish. Like a wishing well. I went out there myself once or twice. Not to wish. Just to test the atmosphere. I found it interesting."

"Yes, it is," I said.

"Well, that's astrology, which you say you know nothing about, although you could learn, and learning, might not scoff." She wagged a finger at me. "But what about astronomy? Anything doing there, eh? Does the old telescope work?"

"It does now," I said. "I've had it repaired."

"Imagine looking through a telescope when the last eyes that looked through the lenses have been dead two hundred years. What have you seen? Anything to report?"

"There is a comet approaching," I said slowly. "A great comet with many tails. It may be visible to the naked eye before the summer is out." Was I really the only person to have looked through Sir Oliver's telescope since his death?

She was enthusiastic. "Oh, very interesting. I suspected we had a little something brewing up. I was getting indications, you know. A comet? Well, that *will* be something."

Simon coughed nervously and at once attracted her attention.

"I don't think Simon looks well," she said, as to the world in general. "It was silly of him to go bathing in the lake. Axwater is old and cold." She made it sound sinister.

"It's been a very hot day," said Simon. "I enjoyed the cold water."

Her sitting room, on the contrary, was overwarm, full

of late Victorian furniture of walnut and damask. Pots of geraniums obscured the windows, and bowls of roses scented the air. The smell of cooking floated in from the kitchen, fragrant and savory. A large tabby cat sat on a chair, eyes closed, swaying slightly as cats do sometimes in self-induced hypnosis. Suddenly the cat's eyes opened.

"Ah, here's the Doctor," said Miss May, who seemed to have hearing as sharp as her cat's.

A second later there was a smart rat-tat on the door: Dr. Montague had arrived. He was a gnarled old tree of a man, upright and unbeaten by the years, although considerably knocked about by them. You got the impression that he had suffered, perhaps by proxy; perhaps he was one of those doctors who absorb the sufferings of their patients. "Brought you a bottle of wine, my dear Grace, to go with the steak and kidney pie. It *is* steak and kidney? Thought I could smell it."

"I can't eat kidney," grumbled Simon. "It makes me feel like Jack the Ripper."

"Leave them, then," snapped Miss May. "James, this is Christabel Warwick."

"Oh, I know all about you," said Dr. Montague, giving my hand a hearty shake.

"Everyone seems to," I said, resigned.

"We are all friends of Piers's here," said Miss May. There was a pause, during which I could hear Dr. Montague's heavy breathing. "That's why we're here. We each have our beggar's mite of information to add to the picture of his death, haven't we, Simon?"

"I've added mine," said Simon.

"Yes. It begins with you. Well, I will go on. I'll offer my bit. I predicted Piers's death. There, that surprises you, doesn't it?"

It didn't surprise me as much as it would have done ten minutes before.

"And I told him," she said.

"I wish you hadn't," I answered. "It might have helped it come true."

"Very true. Very percipient." She nodded her head. "You are sensitive."

"And how did you predict it? Through the stars?"

"They have helped," she admitted.

Dr. Montague said sharply, "Don't include me in your imaginings, Grace. I stick to what I can see."

"Yes, and you may tell that later." She could be sharp in her turn. "No, Christabel, the stars helped: when Betelgueuse approaches Aster, it is always a warning. But the same message came through the letters, and through the cards. The Great Cards," she said reverently. "Tarot."

"Did you tell Piers all this?" I asked.

"Of course, and he laughed."

Dr. Montague said, "Piers took Grace's warnings sufficiently seriously to make a will, which he asked me to witness. I did so, together with my gardener. That is what I have to tell you." He added, "I did not read the contents of the will. Nor do I know what he had to leave, but it is my impression that it benefited you."

"I think Piers was worried about himself anyway," said Simon, "and he didn't need the stars to tell him."

"That may be so," said Grace May peacefully. "The stars do not rule us."

But I was looking at the old doctor. "Piers did not name me though, did he?" I asked. "You cannot be sure I was mentioned in his will at all."

"No. I will tell you what he said. He said to me, 'I have only one thing of value to leave, and I want to make sure it goes to the person I love; it's for her.'"

I nodded. Tears were not far away. I wondered what Piers had left me.

"No will was found," said Dr. Montague. "No will ever has been found."

"Because he destroyed it," said Simon. "That man destroyed it."

"How you do hate Kit Temple," said Grace May. She said it reprovingly, as if he were still a small boy. Then she touched my arm. "My dear, you have every reason to trust to the future."

"Have I?" I said. I suppose I said it sadly, because she looked at me with sympathy and gave my arm quite a sharp pinch. I had already noticed that with Grace May sympathy and love could manifest themselves in hard, awkward ways.

"Bring the wine, James, and we'll go in to supper. You have heard all we've got to say for the moment. After supper we will look for the way forward."

She led us into her dining room, which seemed filled with a huge dining table around which a large Victorian family must once have ranged itself. I felt oppressed; there was too much dark wood for me, too much darkness altogether. I longed to get back to the cool spareness of the observatory. Light and life do go together.

James Montague poured the wine and our hostess served her pie. It tasted delicious; she was a good cook. I couldn't do it justice, though. My mind was full of all the things I had been learning, and it seemed to fill my stomach like indigestible food.

"You're thoughtful, my dear," said the Doctor in a kind voice. "Too pretty a face to wear a frown like that."

"I'm thinking about all I've learned about Piers, and about his death. It's all new to me, you see. All of you have known for months what I have only just learned." I realized I wanted to say something more, fumbled to form the thought and put it into speech. "I haven't learned *enough*. I want to find out more."

The wine was strong, the room warm, I think both were affecting me. Miss May's voice when she spoke seemed to be distant. I felt remote and dreamy. I noticed she had drunk no more wine; her glass remained full.

"After we have eaten we will ask the cards for help."

There was an old-fashioned red-plush cloth on a round table in the living room. Grace May sat herself down, motioned us to sit, and began to lay out her cards.

"Another glass of wine, James? No, none for me. I must keep my senses clear."

She was laying out the pack. Pretty, strange, old-fashioned cards they were.

"The Tarot pack," she said, seeing my eyes on them. "Twenty-two cards, all full of life. And this pack is particularly vigorous. It belonged to my grandmother, and she was a woman who imparted some of her own life to everything she touched, I can tell you."

"Tarot is the most ancient card game in the world," whispered the Doctor to me. "Tarok, it was called originally: the Tarot cards were then the trumps in a fifty-two-card pack. The number of cards in the pack has varied from century to century, it seems."

"The Tarot cards soon emancipated themselves from a mere game of chance," observed Grace May. "They have their own strengths. And much to tell us."

As the cards sped through her hands, I saw the images on the faces: a crowned woman, a man in cap and bells, another man wearing a cloak, a lion, a chariot.

She had laid out nine cards. Not in a circle, nor in regular rows, but first one card on its own, then a row of three, then one card, then a final row of four cards.

She looked at me over them thoughtfully, then closed her eyes as if in prayer. When she opened them again, her eyes were clear and bright, full of command.

"Always remember," she said, "that you rule the cards. You are the mistress, not they. The cards advise only."

I nodded. "I understand," I said, thinking that sometimes what they told must come more like a threat than a warning.

"The cards represent the great elementals, the Platonic ideals. But never think of them as necromancy—the Tarot cards are *good*. What they stand for are the forces of life itself." There was a rapt look on her face, she believed what she was saying. "The Fool, The Magician, The Emperor, we give them these names, but they themselves simply *are*."

Then she began to turn over the cards, slowly and deliberately, pausing for thought between movements, and talking aloud.

"There has been a great disturbance among the cards lately: The Chariot, signifying movement, appearing frequently. I see now this is due to the comet." She nodded her head. "That is satisfactory, a point cleared up. Here's The World again. Not pleased to see that card with us once more. That was the card which principally made me anxious about Piers. Always came with him. And now here it is again." She did indeed sound worried. "By many, it is interpreted as a release from the ordinary physical world and entry into the astral: I take it to mean death. Bother it."

"Grace, I wish you wouldn't," said the Doctor. But I noticed that he kept his eyes on the cards. I guessed he was as interested in the cards as she was. Only Simon looked bored, I suppose because he knew already that all societies had developed techniques for freeing the subconscious mind, and therefore was unsurprised by this one.

Now she was turning the cards over more rapidly. "Ah, here is The Lady. That is you, I believe, Christabel, you have been appearing a good deal lately. Here is The Fool, with us again. How constant he is in attendance. That is significant. But sometimes upright, sometimes upside down. That is another thing that disturbs me: it denotes turmoil." She shook her head. "Here is The Hermit. Seen a lot of him lately. No Chariot this time. Something new is appearing. Yes, someone new is entering the scene." She looked at the card, a wheel with a sphinxlike face above it. "It's The Wheel of Fortune." She shook her head. "But upside down. I don't like it. Something unexpected is going to happen. Perhaps someone is coming. The signs are puzzling. Who or what will come, I cannot say."

After this she put her hands in her lap and looked at me. "There you have it. That is all the cards say today. I simply offer it to you."

"It seems enough," I said.

She put her hand on mine. Hers was warm and dry and firm. "You can call it rubbish if you like. But living as you do in that great center dedicated to the stars, I should not think you would dare."

"But I did not understand it very well."

"If I may paraphrase it then, I think I should say that there are signs of a great turmoil, and that a person of decision could take the initiative. I read the cards with you in mind, and the message is clear, I think: act."

Nothing was clear to me. "And this unexpected thing that is to happen?"

She shrugged. "We shall find out."

Simon stood up. "Come on. I'll take you home. You look tired." He held out his hand to me.

I thanked Grace May for her dinner and, after a moment's thought, for the evening's entertainment.

She laughed. "Oh, you can be skeptical, but you'll

come to trust my beautiful pack of cards. But remember, they can only advise. It is for you to act."

"Oh, I will," I said.

From behind us, as we moved toward the door, I had a winged message to speed me on my way, a whispered, acid breath.

"Leave her alone. Don't push her," I overheard. It was the Doctor.

"I must, James, I must."

I heard him sigh. "Yes, I suppose so. I suppose you must."

I waited, but there was nothing more, only a smile and a nod from the Doctor as we left. I wondered where I was being pushed, and why. Simon and I were silent on the way back. We walked up the footpath through the fields. As we passed the church I turned to look back at the churchyard, silvered beneath the moon. I saw Simon stare searchingly at the sky, as if he hoped to see the great comet.

I was the one who broke the silence. "Have you any idea what Piers left me?" I said.

"No, no idea at all. It wasn't money, anyway. He never had any of that."

"No." We walked on in silence. Simon saw me to the bottom of the path that led to the observatory. I had left lights on in the living room and the stairwell. I saw him look up at them.

"Not nervous?"

"No."

"Nor lonely?"

"Not really." Nor was I.

"Goodnight then. Wave a flag or send up a rocket if you want me, and I'll come running." To my surprise, he bent forward and kissed me gently on the cheek. Then he turned and walked rapidly away.

I went inside and made my way up the winding stair. I locked the door behind me, but the questions that beset me flew in through windows and cracks.

From what I had been told this night, it looked as though Piers had known he might die, and knowing this he had made plans to leave me his sole possession of value. But what this was, or where his will was, I had no idea.

One thing was clear to me: I had to get into Folly House and meet Kit Temple. But how do you get in to see a hermit? I sat there thinking.

My radio contact telephoned me that night. He sounded excited. "I could see the great comet very clearly tonight. It has eight tails. Four long and four shorter ones, arranged symmetrically like a ruff. I'm calling it 'The Lion.'"

"Great name. No, I've not been observing tonight."

"I think the weather's going to change. What is it like with you?"

I glanced toward the window. "Changing here too, I think. The wind's rising."

All through the night the strength of the wind mounted. I could hear it wailing and beating through the trees. In the morning when I got up, the trees were still tossing in the hot dry air. I went down and looked at the lake, which was covered with a white froth.

I didn't go as far as Simon's encampment. Better leave him, I thought. I took a walk through the trees, looking up at their wildly waving leaves, thrashing about, their branches rising and falling with the wind.

I passed the tree, our tree, which Piers and I had used as a letter box.

I could see something white in the hole. Slowly I walked over. I put my hand in and drew out an envelope. It was addressed to me in large square letters: CHRIS.

71

My hand began to shake. The letter inside was brief. The message was short and written in the same square letters.

"I WAS THERE, CHRIS, WHY DID YOU NOT SEE ME? DID YOU NOT SEE ME? TELL ME THE TRUTH. PLEASE TELL ME, CHRISTABEL. I CAME. WHY DID YOU NOT WAIT?"

It was a hot day, but suddenly I was deadly cold. The writing blurred and waved before my eyes as if I were seeing it through water. I forced myself to breathe more slowly. Controlling my pounding heart then, as my eyesight cleared, I read the letter again. "I CAME. WHY DID YOU NOT WAIT?"

It couldn't mean what it said, I told myself incredulously, it couldn't. How could Piers have been there without my seeing him?

In a detached way I saw that my hand was trembling, my fingers shaking as if with an ague. I wanted to hang on to the letter, but the wind jerked at it and snatched at it. Very carefully I folded the paper in two and held it tightly in my hand. I wanted to hang on to it. I wanted to take it home and think about it and work out what it meant.

Did it mean, could it mean, that Piers was alive after all?

Three

When I got back to the observatory I felt sick, literally nauseated, as if someone had kicked me. For the moment I was frightened and ill, at the bottom of the pit with darkness closing in on me. Not hope that Piers was alive, but fear. Then the moment passed. I had dragged myself out of the pit. I knew I had conquered something.

What I had vanquished was unreason. There had to be a rational explanation for this letter; I rallied myself to find it.

I listed all the explanations in my mind. The first, and to my mind the most acceptable, was that it was some unpleasant trick, a sick joke. If I accepted this explanation, then I had to ask myself who had written the letter, pretending to be Piers. It must be someone who knew I had expected to meet Piers. I would have to think further about this point. Piers himself might have told any number of people, people who were faceless to me. I had told

73

no one before the day of our planned meeting, but afterward I had told Tommy in the Creamery Coffee Shop. Simon knew. He might have told someone. I acquitted him of writing the letter. To do so would have been totally out of character.

But perhaps Piers was alive, and the letter *was* from him? In that case I would have to assume the body found on the roadside was not his, never had been his, had been wrongly identified, and that Piers had chosen to let the identification remain, without coming forward. I could not believe this, for it was utterly unlike the Piers I had known. Piers had been simple and straightforward and courageous. Not a person to hide.

But perhaps Piers couldn't help himself?

I put the letter down on the table and stared at it. I wasn't even sure about the handwriting. I had had so few letters from Piers in my time. None of them had I kept. But he had written in a book he had given me. I got up and fetched it.

It was a book of poems: a modest edition of the poems of Robert Burns. Piers had written my name in it, and the date, and a short loving message signed: *Piers*. The letter, perhaps significantly, had not been signed.

I compared the writing of the letter and the writing in the book. I pored over them, laboring at a comparison, trying to be careful, to be as scientific as I could and not jump to any conclusion. At the end I had to admit that I couldn't be sure of anything. I simply couldn't be sure if the same hand had or had not written both messages.

I think at that moment my most profound reaction was that the letter was some kind of rotten trick. Up to now Piers had been the victim. Now I had moved into that position. But all the time a question, a hope remained in my mind.

Meanwhile the winds—which had begun to seem to my

troubled mind like the forces of unreason themselves—still screamed around the tower. A hot sky and a high wind, an unpleasant mixture. The tower seemed to ride out the winds like a ship at sea, but it wasn't an easy day.

Toward evening the wind dropped and the color of the sky faded to a soft turquoise, as though the anger had melted out of it.

I walked down the slope and through the trees. Sky and water seemed to blend together, each catching light and color from the other. Simon was sitting outside his blue tent reading. I went and sat down beside him. I pulled the piece of paper from my pocket and showed it to him.

"This came," I said, watching his face.

He picked it up and studied it. "Came?" he repeated in a bemused way. "How did it come?"

"Perhaps that isn't the right way to put it," I amended. "I found it. In a hole in a tree that Piers and I used as a letter box."

He looked at me in surprise. "You say you found it? Just now?"

"This morning," I said.

He studied it again. "But it looks quite new. Not as if it had lain there for years . . ." His voice trailed away, as if he was beginning to see all the implications at last.

"It hadn't been," I said grimly. "I know that hole was empty. I looked in there the day I was waiting for Piers. No, it's a new letter."

"It says he came, he was there," cried Simon, incredulously.

"It's not signed," I pointed out. "But it pretends to be from Piers. It can't mean anything else. Or so I think."

Simon gave the letter back to me with a wry look. "I should burn it."

75

I took it back. "I might." But I tucked it away in my pocket.

He reached out and took my hand. "It was beastly for you to find," he said gently. "Rotten. Try and forget it. Did it frighten you? It may have been meant to frighten you away."

"No, it didn't frighten me," I said truthfully. I couldn't tell him, couldn't speak, of the terrible hope that was shaping itself in my mind: the hope that perhaps Piers wasn't dead.

Then it was as if he read my thoughts; a brooding look appeared upon his face. "Funny. Grace May predicted a new and unexpected person was going to appear."

"I had noticed," I said.

Our eyes met. I don't know what he read in mine, but I saw worry in his. Anxiety, even.

"We mustn't let her influence our minds," he said. "Although it's hard not to, I admit."

"I don't think she wields such a power over my mind as she may over yours," I observed. "She didn't teach me as a child."

He was scratching his arm; he looked thoroughly uncomfortable. "Is there anything wrong?" I asked.

He sighed. "Some of my equipment is somewhat experimental and I don't manage it very well. The sleeping tent came down on top of me last night. Then my cooking stove blew up. And last, but worst, the gnats and midges down by the lake spent the night nibbling at me."

I looked at him. "Now you mention it, I can see the scars. Why don't you move in with me? Leave your encampment here to use as you like during the day, but you can sleep in the observatory. One of the ground floor rooms is swept and clean. You've got a sleeping bag?"

He accepted gratefully. "Thanks, I do. I will then. Sure you mean it?"

"Yes, you'll be company."

"I'll keep ghosts away, at least." Then he flushed and said awkwardly, "Sorry. I didn't mean that."

"No, of course you didn't." I rose to go, but he pulled me back.

"I'm not usually so awkward, Christabel, believe me. It just seems to be with you. I'd better not come."

"Do you want to come and camp out in the bottom of the observatory?"

"Yes, please."

"Then come, and don't be silly." I got up again, and this time I succeeded in getting away.

I left him standing and watching me go, scratching and looking exasperated with himself.

I climbed up the slope, through the trees, on the other side of Axwater, away from the observatory. At the crest of the hill there was a clearing, a patch of bare turf where not even a shrub grew. Piers used to say that there must have been a neolithic temple on this spot. I don't know if he was right or not. He claimed to have found a little stone phallic symbol there. He said the place was what the Romans would have called *sacra*—and that, in case you don't know, means a place at once holy and cursed. It had *numen*, another word for atmosphere.

From this bare spot you could see the roofs of Folly House. I stood there looking down, thinking. Perhaps the spirit of the place got into me, but I was absolutely determined to find out about Piers and, if necessary, avenge him.

Or, if he was still alive, to rescue him. Rescue? That was a strange word to use.

I realized I had made up my mind that if he *was* still alive, then he must be, in some sense, a prisoner.

It was a fantastic idea and I don't know how it came to me. It seemed to surface from nowhere. I couldn't explain it, even to myself, even while it took root in my mind. "It can't be true," I said to myself. I suppose I wanted it to be true.

And if he was a sort of prisoner, where was he imprisoned? What about considering Folly House for a start? I thought.

I had to get inside it, as an enemy if I had to, but if I could, as a friend.

It proved surprisingly easy. Perhaps it was the cards. They had predicted the arrival of someone unexpected on the scene; they had announced turmoil and change; through the mouthpiece of Grace May they had told me to act. They hadn't said that they were working away quietly to help me, but I think they must have been.

This time their mouthpiece was Dr. Montague, and I suppose his closeness to Grace May should have made me ask if the cards were totally disinterested in their help.

In the cool of the evening I took some letters down to the post office in the village. The wind had dropped, and I found the walk pleasant. In his front garden, attending to his roses, I saw Dr. Montague. He waved his hand at me. Then he cut a deep-red rose and gave it to me. I took it and tucked it into my waist, where it looked like blood.

"Roses and jeans," he said with a smile. "It would have been chiffon or muslin once. Tucked lawn, my mother wore in the summer. Glad to see you. You said you wanted to meet Kit Temple."

"And you said it was difficult."

"Go and have a look at an advertisement in the window of the village store," he said cheerfully. "The gods have made it easier for you." Yes, he actually said those words. "I think it'll fit you. It might almost have been made for you. Go and have a look."

The village store was an old-fashioned shop. One side window was stuck with handwritten and typed cards offering goods and services for sale from one set of people, side by side with urgent requests for similar objects and services from another set of people. Whether they ever got matched up seemed doubtful. It looked as though no one ever read anyone else's advertisement.

I hadn't much difficulty finding the card to which Dr. Montague had drawn my attention. It was the newest card there, clean and unspotted.

TUITION IN MATHEMATICS TO UNIVERSITY STANDARD REQUIRED.
APPLY TEMPLE
FOLLY HOUSE

I read it through again, although it was simple enough to take in: to understand it was another matter.

Someone in Folly House wanted to learn mathematics? How strange, and how fortuitous.

Now I could get into Folly House. I ardently wanted to. As I stood there reading the advertisement, Grace May appeared. She saw what I was doing and nodded with satisfaction.

"Strange how things work out, is it not? That card only appeared this morning, but already I see it as part of the chain of life. Into which you will fit." She gave me an appraising glance. "No, let me see, I should say you were a Leo, yes, a typical Leo, with all their spunk. Now that the opening has come, you will take it. I never doubted you for a moment."

"I suppose I can apply," I observed. "That's not the same as being accepted."

Grace May just smiled. "It's all there, my dear, one has only to read the signs." Then she added practically,

"How many people do you suppose can teach mathematics around here?"

The denial of free will thus wished upon me jointly by Grace May and the stars irked me. I turned away. "I'm not at all sure I shall apply. I have plenty of other things to do."

Behind me I heard her laugh gently.

"Don't leave it till morning," she called after me. "Go now. The night is the time."

"The night is the time." I repeated the words to myself as I walked through the trees. The night is the time for what?

An elegant set of cast-iron railings ran through the woods, separating the land belonging to Folly House from the land belonging to the observatory. The rails were old and beautiful, but by no means in good repair. Here and there came gaps where some of the sentinel rails had fallen and the grass and weeds grown over them. Here and there animals had pushed through and trampled on them. Tracks in the grass leading down to Axwater were clearly paths used daily by animals going down to drink in the lake.

Like an animal, I meant to follow such a track and make my secret way to Folly House.

I pushed through a gap in the railings. Judging by the tawny hairs still adhering to one of the rails, the last creature through had been a fox. As quietly as Reynard himself, I slipped through into the woods beyond. How rich this place was, I thought, in animals and vegetation and associations. There was Axwater, ageless and deep; there was the clearing on the hill, so full of mystery; there were the woods themselves, immemorially old; and there were the two buildings which seemed in a strange kind of way to vie with each other—the old observatory and Folly House.

One I already knew intimately. I had entered into its life and it had come into mine. Now I was about to encounter the other place: Folly House.

Here the path was steeper and more slippery than on the other side and I found myself slithering and falling. I steadied myself by grabbing at the branch of a tree. The leaves parted, and I found myself staring into a startled gray face: a small squirrel had been disturbed in his sleep. He jumped lightly away and was gone.

Now I could observe the house clearly. A gap in the trees allowed a view straight through to it. I saw now why it was called Folly House. It was a Chinese folly, a small, stucco-faced English country house, built about eighteen-thirty, the roof ornamented with little frills and curls pretending to make it look like a pagoda. It was a very pretty joke.

The Folly was framed in formal gardens, which even from where I stood looked overgrown and neglected. The Chinese influence had extended here too, and a tiny red pavilion stood in the garden, surrounded by a miniature vista of waterfalls leading to tiny pools ringed with delicate flowering shrubs.

I continued to walk down the slope. The closer I got to the house, the quieter it looked and the more closed in on itself. Very soon I came to a stretch of open parkland lightly dotted with elms and beeches. I suppose I could now have been seen myself, but there seemed to be no one about to see me.

I walked round the edge of the Chinese garden, taking a broad stone-flagged path, which was covered with fallen rose petals, to the walls of the house itself. I could see the front door round a corner. A pretty and elegant entrance it was, with a fanlight shaped like a shell above the door and a curving sweep of six steps, with a balustrade of worked iron that reminded me of the railings to the park.

A row of three windows faced me, equally spaced along one wall. Pale yellow curtains edged each window. I went up close and looked inside. A book-lined room, obviously a library, was there before me. A desk neatly arranged for work lay directly beneath one window. In another was a round library table covered with books and periodicals. The third window contained a seat covered with what looked to be a white fur rug. The room appeared quite empty.

I was standing looking in when the white fur rug reared up, separated into three parts, and burst into a fury of barks. Three angry Pekingese faces appeared simultaneously at the windowpanes, exploding with noise. I had met them once already; they hadn't liked me much then, and they seemed to like me no better now.

But they had drawn attention to me and as I walked round the corner of the house I was not surprised to see the front door slowly open. The dogs rushed out, followed by their master.

"Good evening, Miss Warwick," said Kit Temple.

"Good evening," I said nervously. "We've met before. In the woods."

"I remember," he said, a trifle grimly, I thought.

"I didn't know who you were then, of course." I must have sounded nervous.

He had got himself in hand. "I am afraid I was irritable that day. I apologize. Not your fault. Just something you reminded me of."

I waited, but he wasn't going to say any more. I thought I could finish the sentence, however, at least to my own satisfaction. I reminded him of his nephew, Piers. I thought he must have known, or guessed, of my connection with his nephew.

The dogs were silent now, sitting a few inches from their master's heels, a quiet, watchful bunch.

"I came in answer to your advertisement," I said to this hostile group.

Kit Temple's eyebrows shot up. "*You* did?" he asked. "I see. Well, that's a bit of a surprise."

"You were serious? In earnest about needing a tutor for mathematics?"

"Oh, dead serious." He thought about it for a while, and then said, almost to himself, "I'm serious all right."

"Then who's it for?" I said. "Who needs the coaching? Who is the pupil?"

"I do. I am the pupil."

I was neither surprised nor unsurprised. "Then I am the teacher who offers herself."

The dogs stood up, as if I had said something important. But I soon saw that it was really in answer to a small movement of their master's hand. "Come inside," he said gravely. "We'll talk it over." Over his shoulder he said, "Come on, dogs." But of course, they were already moving ahead of him, a beady-eyed set of guardians.

At the door I hesitated, looking warily at those three sets of perfectly working teeth. He saw my face and read it accurately. There was no denying his intelligence.

"Take no notice of the dogs, they're a friendly bunch really."

Oh yes? I thought. Aloud I said, "Will they bark?"

"They won't bark as you come in, only as you leave." He stood aside to let me enter. "Sit, Drusus. Down, Nero. Quiet, Agrippa." Drusus and Agrippa seemed to have a relationship which, if they were kin, was incestuous, and was in any case frankly amorous. Nero, although as white as the other two, had a black patch over one eye, which had no doubt earned him his name.

"Are those really their names?"

"Their formal names," he assured me, without a flicker

83

of a smile. "I have shorter names for when I'm in a hurry. Come in, come in."

I followed him. I was inside Folly House.

We were standing in a square hall flagged in black and white. There was a low dark oak chest in one corner, a mirror above it decorated with cupids, and a fine old Persian rug on the floor.

Without another word he led me into the room I had already named the library; as he went he was switching on lamps.

"The light's fading," he said. "It's been a long day." He sounded tired. "Well, come on then, what's this about teaching me mathematics?"

The aggressive approach, after the gentleness, threw me off balance. He seemed to be a man of moods, moved to easy yet not easily explained irritations.

"You advertised," I said coldly. "I'm quite competent to do it. If you don't want me or aren't serious about it after all, I'll go away."

"You'll hear some strange stories about me in the village, I expect." He said it without rancor, almost as if he was amused.

"You seem respected," I said.

"Old Mother May, the old witch, doesn't care for me, for one. We've clashed and I've come out on top." No doubt about the amusement now. He sat down on a sofa whose rumpled cushions suggested it was his usual seat. "Have a drink. What would you like? It's late enough in the day for brandy, but too hot, I think. I've got some nice cool hock." He rose stiffly.

"People are always offering me drinks around here," I said, and I sounded pettish in my turn. He looked at me and laughed.

"You can always say no."

The trouble was I wasn't Catherine's sister for nothing, and the hock sounded delicious. "I am hot, so I'll say yes."

In a little while he came back with two tall green glasses on a silver tray and the slender bottle. He poured me a glass and handed it to me. "You're Christabel Warwick, and an ancestor of yours originally built the old observatory, and last year your brother-in-law bought it and did it up. So you belong round here, yet you have a slight but distinct American accent."

"I'll soon lose it now I'm home."

"Oh, you will?" He gave me a smile. "Don't try too hard. It's charming. I shall enjoy learning about the higher calculus in a Boston accent."

I frowned slightly. "It's not Boston, is it?" It probably was, though; my best friend at Bryn Mawr had been a girl from Boston. We had been much together. "I've got the job then, have I?"

"Unless you drive too hard a bargain." He was still smiling.

"I won't do that." My voice was not quite as steady as I would have wished. I had already noticed his likeness to Piers. What I had not expected was the sheer, physical impact of it on me. He was so like Piers, like Piers grown older, but with all his vitality, even though some of the humor and sensitivity was not there.

In spite of myself, in spite of everything, a little sliver of ice in my heart melted. I took a deep breath, determined not to let my resolve weaken.

"You'll find me a good pupil," he said, then added, "as far as I'm able." He took a deep breath. And I waited, waited for something more to come, but that was all, he'd said what he wanted to say.

"Yes, well, that brings me to something. How much math have you done, and how far do you want to go?" I was curious.

"I've covered the elementary stuff, of course—that is how I know I want to go on," he said with composure. "It suits me, I find."

"And the reference to 'university level,' does that mean you are thinking of going on to a university?" I was, if anything, even more curious after listening to his explanations.

His composure matched my curiosity. "No, I only used that phrase to indicate that I wanted to go as far as I could."

"As far as you could?" I took a deep breath, thinking it a strange phrase.

"Time is the factor there," he said, in a level voice. "I am not sure how much time I shall have to give to it."

"I can certainly give what you want in the way of instruction," I said, my eyes taking in the room around me. The walls were painted a deep olive green and decorated with coaching prints that looked genuine. The armchairs and sofa were covered in tan leather, with the exception of one chair of chrome and hide that was straight out of the Bauhaus, and which also seemed genuine and not somebody's yesterday's imitation. There was something about the nuts and bolts which looked in period and forty-five years old. The library table had been built in the eighteenth century by a craftsman for a gentleman's library. It was a conventional room with one or two unorthodox surprises, like the Bauhaus chair, and the display (I thought you could call it that) stretched along one wall.

There was a chessboard with the pieces laid out. A card table stood next to it with a game of patience set out on a surface that looked more suited to bridge. By the card table a backgammon board stood as if ready to be used. Other objects that I did not really recognize but clearly associated with games of chance were assembled nearby.

He saw me looking at them and smiled. "Yes, mathematics seems an appropriate learning for a gambler, doesn't it?"

I nodded. "Is that why you are doing it?"

"I suppose that's where it started. I was looking for something to occupy my mind, fill it up with no room to spare. I thought mathematics would do that better than a study of history or philosophy."

"So it's just the best way to pass the time?"

"Yes, that's it, a way to pass the time." Again he smiled at me. "Very suitable too. The whole universe is just a numbers game, isn't it?"

"So the physicists say," I answered, more than ever perplexed by him.

"Yes, a study of pure numbers will do me very well. Have some more hock?" He was being generous to me, but I had noticed that he did no more than sip his own drink.

"No, thank you. Shall we settle when I shall come for the first session?" I looked at him. "You *do* want me to come here? If not, you could come to the observatory."

"And work under old Sir Oliver's skeptical aegis? Now there *was* a mathematician, and I shall only be stumbling in his footsteps."

"You'd be surprised how far mathematics has gone in two hundred years," I observed. "Tomorrow then?"

"Yes, at what time? I prefer the morning if that suits you." I nodded. "Good. And we have to settle the fee."

"I shan't be grasping."

He smiled. "No, I'm sure you won't."

I was looking about me. He seemed to have some lovely possessions. At one end of a low bookcase stood a very beautiful Chinese jar. About ten inches high, the porcelain was glazed a soft egg-shell blue and it was decorated in rouge-de-fer and green enamels with flowering trees, animals and human figures. I found myself studying the figures. I could make out that one was an old man, very tall and wearing a towering headdress; another was a young man, short-tunicked and slender; and the third was a girl. The girl and the boy stood side by side and the old man towered over them. On the obverse side the boy lay on the ground, the girl bent over him, huge almond tears suspended from her eyes, and the old man still stood where he was. I amused myself by fancying it told a story of two young lovers and a Mandarin magician. I looked to the other end of the bookcase expecting to find its mate, but there was nothing.

Kit Temple saw my look. "The other one's gone," he said briefly.

"Then there was a pair?"

"There was indeed."

"And you've lost it? Oh, what a shame."

"Yes, it was a pity," he said, and his voice was grim. The look he gave me was unexpected because full of a question. It almost seemed as if I was expected to *know*.

"They look valuable."

"Very valuable," he said. "A pair of vases signed by an artist called Wan Li who worked in the late sixteenth century. They're not priceless, but they are valuable. I wish I could sell them, but—"

Before he could say any more, the telephone began to ring in another room. It sounded some distance away. We both waited, but it went on ringing.

"Well?" I raised an eyebrow and looked at him.

"Yes, I'll have to go and answer that telephone. Please excuse me, I'll be back shortly."

I did wait a few minutes after he had gone, then I went quietly to the door. The three dogs watched me silently and without moving, although as I touched the door one of them gave a low warning growl. I closed the door swiftly behind me and waited to see if the dogs would begin to bark. Silence.

So much for them, I thought, and looked around me. The hall was empty. I could hear Kit Temple's voice, but distantly, as if several rooms separated us. Across the hall I could see a closed door and at the back of the hall, under the curve of the staircase, an archway leading to a passage. I think the telephone was down this passage.

I opened the closed door and looked into the room beyond. The light from the hall showed me that it was darkened and shut-up. The stale smell of dead air told me that it had been shut for weeks, perhaps months. The furniture seemed to be shrouded in white sheets as if it had been thrust into limbo.

I closed the door and drew back into the hall. I could still hear Kit's voice. In front of me stretched the staircase with its treads, wide, shallow and tempting. Tempting me to run up them and look around upstairs.

Then I was running up the stairs, my heart bumping.

At the top I was confronted by a broad landing with doors set in the walls on either side of the staircase, and three in the wall opposite.

I tried them one after the other. Then I turned and went back to the staircase. I walked swiftly down the stairs, getting back to the hall just in time to be standing there as Kit Temple hurried back.

"Oh, there you are," he said. "Sorry I was such a long time."

"I'm just going."

As if they had heard me, the dogs started to bark. "They always know," he said. "Very well, if you are coming back tomorrow, I'll give you a key."

"A key?"

"Yes, to the front door. Then you can let yourself in. This is a very shut-up house."

As I accepted the key and walked away, promising to return tomorrow, I felt like laughing hysterically.

Yes, it was a very shut-up house. And yes, I did need a key. Many keys.

I walked away fast. There was something terribly strange about this house, a desolation at its core. Every door on the upper floor had been locked.

A crackle of lightning flashed across the sky, as if the elements were joining in.

Four

That night, as soon as I returned to the observatory, I could see by the lights shining from the tower and a pair of climbing boots on the steps that Simon had arrived.

He appeared as soon as I entered, carrying a bottle of milk in one hand and a pair of socks in the other. "I shall be comfortable here," he said, shuffling his bare feet on the stone of the steps as if it burned him. "Thanks. And I won't get in your way." Then he saw I was carrying a large key. "What's that?"

"The key to Folly House. I'm going back tomorrow."

"You don't let the grass grow under your feet. I hope you know what you're doing. And you've actually got a key? Well, I never."

"Yes. I don't think he's got any servants there at all. That's strange, isn't it?"

Simon frowned. "Yes, I'd say it was. I hope you'll be all

right in the place." He sounded uncertain. "He's much liked in the village, you know. They think he's a great man."

"I believe he wants me there, and I didn't get the impression he suspects me of any untoward purpose."

"He's not stupid," warned Simon. "Or he used not to be."

"And he isn't now," I said, recalling the look of luminous intelligence on Kit Temple's face. "But neither am I. Don't worry."

He was studying me. "You look tired."

"I expect I do. A practicing amateur astronomer and detective combined doesn't get much sleep." I yawned. "I shan't be watching tonight. The comet will have to wander a little farther into our skies without me watching it."

"Doesn't it frighten you?" he said.

"No." But it wasn't quite true. I did get a strange feeling when I thought about that wanderer in the heavens, endlessly and forever, as far as one knew, circling the universe. Whose eyes had watched it when it had last come near the earth? Had man been here at all? Would he be here when it came back? Unknowable answers to impossible questions. Perhaps it would never come back. Comets did break up and disappear. "Would you like some coffee?"

He nodded and followed me up the stairs to my kitchen, padding softly now on the thick carpet. He showed every sign of settling in with me as comfortably as a cat.

I started the coffee and put out a tin of biscuits. Simon took one at once and ate it in two bites; then he started to sort through the biscuits looking for one covered in chocolate. "Make these yourself, did you?" he said through an appreciative mouthful.

"Yes." I was watching the coffee. "They're easy."

"Clever girl." He reached out for another one. "You might teach me. Men ought to cook."

I poured the coffee. "Simon, I keep thinking about the bequest Piers left me. I wish I knew what it was and why I haven't had it. Do you think I could ask his uncle?"

"No," said Simon.

"Not straightaway, I mean, but leading up to it. I think I might learn something."

"Such as what?"

"Such as whether Piers *is* dead," I said. "Or alive."

"What?" Simon's hand dropped from the biscuit tin.

"I see a lot of importance in that bequest. If I knew more about what it was, I believe I would know also about other things."

"You don't really mean that, about Piers, do you?" he said hesitantly. "I mean, what you said. About him being alive?"

"I don't know. I have such a strange feeling. I'm trying to find a reason for it." I stared into my coffee.

"Oh, Chris." Simon took my hand. "He's dead. You have to believe it. I spoke to the policeman who saw him."

"I believe he saw someone he thought was Piers," I said, not withdrawing my hand but not clasping his either. "Perhaps it wasn't him, though."

"Oh, my dear," he began. "I'm sure."

"I'm not sure of anything," I said. "Did anyone else identify him? He was terribly injured, you know."

"His uncle did, I suppose," said Simon.

"Apart from him?" I said.

Simon shook his head. "Not that I heard."

"I wish I knew," I said, getting up. "Suppose Piers is *not* dead."

"Oh, Chris, don't deceive yourself."

"Someone's deceiving me." I stood up.

93

"I love you, Chris." Simon stood up too.

"Don't say that."

He sank back into his seat. "Sorry," he muttered. "Wrong time, wrong place." The lines of his face looked angry. He's got a rotten temper, I thought, when he doesn't get what he wants. Too much of that, I thought, and we should soon quarrel.

He couldn't leave it there, though; he knew he should, but he couldn't do it. "I do love you. Yes, I can see in your face you don't want me to say it. Don't welcome me as a lover, in fact."

"Oh, Simon," I protested.

"Yes, I can hear that note in your voice. *Poor* Simon. You're sorry for me. Perhaps you're even enjoying it a bit."

"No."

"I don't know that I'd blame you. It wouldn't be unnatural; I might even be pleased. At least I'd be amusing you."

"I don't laugh at you, Simon, I promise. I think of you as a good, sweet, kind person."

"That means you think nothing of me at all."

"No, it doesn't," I cried.

"Not in the way I want," he finished with some bitterness.

He stared at me, his expression half aggressive, half hurt. And miraculously, at that moment a tiny spark of emotion flared between us. He saw it; I dropped my eyes.

But the thing had happened, and I knew that although I might want to forget it, he would not.

Slowly and very delicately he put out his hand and held my fingers, stroking them one after the other. Then he quietly took his hand away. I knew I would have to reckon now with more force and subtlety in Simon than I had bargained for. But why did it have to be a sort of battle between us, as I sensed it was?

To break the moment, I said, "Do you remember anything about the object that Piers was leaving me, 'the only object of value' he said he owned? Did he describe it? Or even hint what it was?"

Simon shook his head. "No. He just said he'd picked it up. In some street market or junk shop, I suppose. He didn't talk about it. I don't really want to."

In the morning I took my key and went to Folly House. I was early, the house seemed asleep. But the dogs were awake—a wide-eyed triangle lying looking at me in the hall. All silent, however.

Kit's voice called to me from the library. "In here."

He was half sitting, half lying, on the big sofa, wearing a formidable Chinese dressing gown and reading the morning papers.

"Good morning." He stood up politely. You can always tell a person who has had little sleep, and I saw at a glance that he had had less than I.

"Here's the syllabus." I tossed a sheet of paper across to him. "Is it what you want? Everything from the calculus differential and integral to differential geometry. All neatly laid out and listed."

He read, smiled and commented, "Hmm . . . the theory of sets. Cantor's paradox . . . yes, I've heard of that. . . . The axiom of reducibility . . . the simple theory of types . . . Whitehead, Russell . . . Quine. I know the names."

"A bit more than that, I hope," I said drily.

He looked up at me and smiled. "Yes, a bit more. I see you mean to take me all the way."

"Oh yes, I shall stretch you." I got a sort of satisfaction in saying that.

Still studying what I had written, he said, "I'll need some books. I see you've given me a book list."

"Yes, you might as well study the philosophy of mathematics."

"Oh yes, the philosophy," he said thoughtfully. The dogs had come into the room and ranged themselves round him, pretending to sleep. "One or two of the books I have. Russell, for instance, the *Principia Mathematica*." He nodded to the bookshelves behind him. "Others I can order."

"I'll try the library in Brayford," I said. "I'll go over today." Then I said deliberately, "Or you could go yourself." I was testing him out. Would he go, or was he really a hermit?

"No," he said. "No. I don't propose to go out." He didn't say it with any special emphasis, but I knew without being told that he had made a statement of importance.

"Right. I'll go for you. Meanwhile, I did bring this book with me and you can study these pages and do these problems." I flipped through the pages of the book I had brought with me and handed it to him. "I've marked the passages. See how it goes, it will at least show me where to start."

He accepted it obediently: the teacher-pupil relationship was established. Again I was conscious of pleasure.

We talked for a few more minutes, dogs listening intently, attentive scholars, then I made a move to go. On the table in the window I noticed a colored feather mop. I wondered if he used it for dusting.

He saw me looking and smiled. "Do you live here all by yourself?" I said.

"A woman comes up from the village twice a week to clean, and as you can see, I do a little dusting myself. I don't like her in here. Well, not too much. It's disturbing."

Again that strange note of self-isolation. "You've got a lot of land as well," I said. "That needs looking after."

"There is one man who tends the trees. A forester, I suppose you could call him. The flower gardens"—he used the slightly archaic idiom with a complete lack of self-consciousness—"well, they are steadily going to seed, as I expect you have noticed."

"I had noticed," I assented.

He did not let me go without a little inquisition of his own. He took me to the door of the library, dogs attendant, and paused. I knew something was coming.

"You were my nephew's girl friend, weren't you?" His voice was quiet and cool, but some fire burned behind his eyes.

I was caught off guard. "I thought no one knew," I said after a pause. As we stood, close together, our eyes were almost level. I could see my own image reflected in his.

"I knew. Of course I knew. Don't stare. When you look alarmed like that, your eyes are as amber as your hair. I've never seen eyes of quite that color."

"Light brown," I said. I felt winded, as if my heart had stopped.

"I prefer amber." And he smiled.

From outside I heard the shuffle of footsteps and the rattle of china. In came an aged, bent figure wearing a faded blue apron and carrying a tray. "It's Mrs. Gamble," said Kit.

"Brought you a cup of coffee," announced Mrs. Gamble. "Thought the young lady might like a cup. Just having one myself." On the tray was one delicate dark blue and gold Crown Derby cup and saucer, a thick white mug, a well polished silver coffee pot, and a pudding basin full of sugar lumps. "The cup's for the lady," direct-ed Mrs. Gamble. "I know you like your old mug."

"Keeps the coffee hotter," agreed Kit amiably.

She poured the coffee, the cup delicate as eggshell to me, the mug to Kit Temple. "Come on now, Mr. Kit, drink up." There was a kind of harsh benevolence in her tone. She hardly glanced at me. For her I only existed in relationship to Kit Temple. If I pleased him, that suited her.

I refused a sugar lump and sipped my coffee: it was very hot and very strong. A satisfied smile played round Mrs. Gamble's mouth as she watched her employer drink. I noticed that she had a faint but noticeable mous-tache of fine red hair. Her figure had been bent over by years of hard manual work, and there was a thick, gnarled look to her hands, as if they knew what it was to be used for heavy, hard labor. Nothing daunted or tired in her gaze, though, I thought; her eyes were lively and alert. In one pocket of her blue overall she had thrust a yellow duster, and next to the yellow duster was a big bunch of keys.

My eyes rested on those keys. They looked like the keys to the whole of Folly House. In the bunch she must have the keys to the locked rooms upstairs. I wondered where the keys were kept when she wasn't wearing them, and whether I could get possession of them.

My thoughts were broken into by Kit Temple. "Give me about four days to do this work, will you? I know my own speed."

"Sure." I nodded. "And I'll go to the library in Bray-ford as I promised. Four days from now, then? I'll be back."

Oh yes, I thought. I'll be back.

The dogs waited till I had the front door open and then started to bark. This little habit of theirs would certainly be a problem for anyone trying to leave the house secretly.

I had a key; I could enter Folly House whenever I wished. But the dogs would never let me out. I could almost see the faint smile on Kit Temple's face. He knew what he was about when he handed me the key. He had his protectors.

Was it possible he was watching me, as I was watching and testing him?

Kit Temple was an enigma to me. On the surface he seemed an attractive, thoughtful person, a man to like and respect. But all the time I caught a brooding, puzzling undertone to his character, a mysterious quality that puzzled me. Certainly he kept a strange ménage in Folly House.

Anyway, I did what I said I would do: I went to the county library in Brayford. There I found a few of the books I wanted, though not many. The subject was poorly represented in the library, which did not surprise me. England is not a mathematical country.

But while I was there I saw a large rack of newspapers, including all the London daily papers, and this display gave me an idea.

I would advertise. I sat at one of the tables there and decided what I would say. I was deeply anxious to discover more about this object of value that Piers had "picked up." It had to have come from somewhere, and my guess was from somewhere not too far away. Objects of value have a past and history. This one would have had other owners and would be remembered by them. One of them might have sold it to Piers. Yes, the implication of the phrase "picked up" was that he had *bought* it and not been given it.

I had the strong feeling that finding out something about this object would tell me something more about

Piers. If I knew what the object of value was that he had destined for me, I might be able to guess why he had wanted me to have it. I still would not know why I had not received it; I still would not know what had really happened to Piers; but what I thought, almost without being willing to admit it, was that the advertisement would stir things up.

Someone would know I was taking an active interest in Piers. It would be a stone thrown in the pool.

I drew a piece of paper toward me and started to scribble down what I wanted to say. The question, the request and my telephone number. No mention of my name, only Piers's.

I had just about finished when I realized someone was standing at my elbow. I looked up to meet the librarian's wide and enthusiastic smile. Perhaps it wasn't really enthusiasm, I reflected, but simply the curve of her cheeks and her round blue eyes that made her seem so. There was no mistake about her friendliness, though.

"Alba Bailey," she said. "That's my name. Christabel Warwick, isn't it? Nice to see you again. Did you find what you wanted?"

I nodded.

"I am glad to see you again. Remember our discussion group I told you about? I've had a little talk with our president, Grace May, and she's suggested I should definitely ask you to give us a talk about the observatory and also ask if we could have our meeting on the site, so to speak, in the tower. Oh, it would be so nice. We're so interested in the stars at the moment. We usually take a theme, you know." Her nice, kind face lost its smile and edged toward a frown. "I never know whether to take the stars seriously or not. But sometimes I feel, yes, they are influencing my life, I sense their power." She shook her head as if to dispel the stellar influence. "I don't *want* to believe, but do you know, I think I do." She looked at me questioningly. "Do you believe?"

I shrugged.

"Yes, I'm like that, I suppose, can't quite make up my mind. How are you getting on with Mr. Temple?"

"Fine," I said, not surprised that she knew about this too. I suppose everyone in Steeple Minden and quite a few in Brayford knew I was tutoring Kit Temple.

"Clever man," she said. "Oh, he was so full of wit and life once. You could see vitality shining out of him. He was so attractive."

"He still is," I said, reluctantly.

"But changed," she said. "Oh, he is changed. He doesn't seem the same man. I wonder what caused it. I wonder all the time. Of course, one never sees him now," she ended sadly. She met my interested eyes and a pinkness rose in her cheeks. "I did like him. Not that he ever gave me any cause to hope. Oh well, that's the way it goes." She ended with a sigh.

A little tentative growth of friendship was beginning to spring up between us. I liked her. "You must visit the observatory," I said. I could hear my voice picking up and imitating her own enthusiastic note. "Let's set a date. Say two weeks from today?"

She consulted her diary. "That's August 28th. It's all right for me. I'm on duty here all day, but free in the evening. Sometimes I'm responsible for opening our small branch library in the evening—there's one in Steeple Minden that's open every Monday. I'll have to consult Miss May."

The oracle again, I thought.

Within a week my advertisement started appearing, first in two London newspapers, then later in the country weeklies. Then silence. No response came from anyone except my employer, if you could call Kit Temple that, and he raised the subject with me in his own way.

At the end of our next session he stood up in a manner I was now beginning to recognize as the preliminary to something.

"What's this about advertising for something of value sold to my nephew?" His face was grim.

I stood up. I had so far found no opportunity to continue my search of the house. I considered what to say.

"I was told that Piers had left me something of value in his will. I have never received it. I thought I would like to know more," I said, a grim note creeping into my voice, too.

"I have never even heard of a will," said Kit Temple. "I don't believe there was one. Piers had nothing to leave."

I was silent.

"You could have spoken to me about it," he said irritably. "I would have told you."

I still did not answer.

"Why didn't you?"

I shrugged. "It puzzled me. Worried me, if you like. I feel I don't know what happened to Piers."

In a tight voice he said, "You are making a mystery of something where there is no mystery, only a terrible tragedy. And God knows there has been enough of that in my family. Forget it. Leave it. You are creating stories for yourself."

I flushed. "We'll see," I said.

"Piers is dead," he said. "Can't you leave him dead? Must you make romances out of it for yourself?"

I hated him then. I gathered my books and papers together. I would have liked to leave him then forever and never come back. But I couldn't do that. I had not finished with Folly House. I was more determined than ever to keep a footing there. "I'll see you the day after tomorrow, as we arranged," I said, keeping my voice level.

I knew we had crossed a kind of Rubicon in our relationship. We had crossed swords. I doubted he trusted me now.

At the door I looked back: he was slumped on the sofa, eyes gazing out the window toward the hills. I didn't read anger or hostility in that figure, but a sort of despair.

That evening the telephone rang in my living room at the observatory. I picked it up, thinking it might be Catherine or Iris. I thought I wouldn't mind hearing from Catherine, who had been silent and noncommunicative lately. I missed her.

"Christabel Warwick speaking."

"Oh, Miss Warwick, is it you?" I heard a woman's voice, pleasant and well-educated. "I didn't realize. . . ." She sounded flustered.

"Yes, what is it?" I asked. "Who is it speaking?"

"Barbara New of Mallards. It's about your advertisement. I didn't know whether to ring. You only quoted a number, you see. I didn't know it was *you*."

I didn't understand. I didn't know her, but she seemed to know me. "What do you mean? If you know something about Piers Temple's treasure, please tell me. It's what I asked." And then suddenly the implication of something she had said got through to me. "Mallards, you said? Mallards!"

Mallards was one of the smaller London auction rooms, not so large or famous as Sotheby's or Agnew's, but distinguished. Surely Piers had not picked up his valuable possession at Mallards?

"Yes, you know I'm at Mallards." A note of exasperation surfaced in her voice. "We sold a small bronze figure of a goddess, of unknown origin but probably dating from

103

1000 to 500 B.C., once the property of Piers Temple." Now her voice was frosty. "That's why I answered your advertisement, although frankly I am surprised it was *you*."

"Why?" My voice was sharp. "Who sold the statuette?"

"Why, *you* did, Miss Warwick," said the woman. "It fetched two thousand guineas."

"*No*." I only breathed the denial over the telephone, my voice knocked out of me by shock.

"You telephoned me in May to make the arrangements, and in June the statue was auctioned. It fetched a higher price than I expected because it was beautiful."

"No, no I *didn't*." I had got my voice back. "I did *not*."

"You said you were Christabel Warwick on the telephone, and your letter of receipt was signed," she said bleakly, "C. Warwick. I remembered, and that's why I telephoned. Now I wish I hadn't; I don't quite know what it's all about, Miss Warwick, but I'd rather know no more."

But I had thought of something important. "How did you know that the bronze which this person who called herself a name not her own was selling had any connection with Piers Temple? Did she say so?"

There was a perceptible pause and then she said, "No. As it happened, I had seen the piece before."

"What?" I was nonplussed. "Where?"

"I don't remember exactly." She seemed ready to end the conversation. I didn't believe her for a moment.

"Don't ring off," I said quickly. "No, please don't. Can we meet to talk? I live near Brayford." I knew that I could not let her get away before I'd found out all that she knew; at least I had found a chink in the mystery surrounding Piers and his death. "I'll come to London to meet you."

If necessary I would penetrate the sacred halls of Mallards and see her there; I suppose she heard the determination in my voice, because when she spoke again her voice was less hostile.

"No, don't do that," she said slowly. "I'll come to see you. I have to see a client in that part of the country on Friday. I know where Brayford is."

"Right. We'll meet in Brayford. In two days' time. Will you drive or come by train?"

She hesitated, then said, "I'll drive."

"Then I will meet you at the Creamery Coffee Shop in Brayford. It's in the Market Square."

Again she hesitated. "The Creamery Coffee Shop," she said. "At noon."

"I'll be there. No, wait a minute. Do you still believe it was I who spoke to you on the telephone back in May?"

"I recognized your voice," she said immediately.

"Yes, I know you did. But was the voice really identical? Do I sound quite the same?"

"You are talking differently. There's an accent I don't remember noticing. But it may have been there." She was hesitant again. "But I knew your voice." She sounded puzzled and uneasy.

I wondered if she really would come to meet me, so I tried to make certain. "You will come? Are you sure that you wouldn't rather come to the old observatory in Steeple Minden? That's where I live. I have a special reason for wanting to talk to you."

There was a pause; I thought she wasn't going to answer. Then: "I too have a special reason," she said. "And I know where you live, Miss Warwick. You forget that is where I sent the check for the sale."

It was a bad moment, one of the worst, and I was coming to be a specialist in bad moments. Lately they had come in a cluster. There is a mathematical theory of clusters, and I was beginning to feel like a digit living in the midst of one. First there had been the moment when I learned of Piers's death; then the moment when I was told it was murder; and there was the moment when I read the strange letter that suggested he was not dead. For some reason this moment, when I was told that I had sold Piers's treasure, his gift to me, and that I had already received a check for it, had a peculiar nastiness all its own. It seemed to be drawing me right into the heart of the mystery about Piers, as if I had, unknown to myself, played a part in it. The moment descended on me sickeningly, a chilling, frightening moment.

In all my life I had never been a girl for confidences: I didn't talk over my problems much even to myself. I suppose this is what had made it easy for me to set up my original tryst with Piers and to hug my secret to myself. But now I badly wanted to talk to someone.

It was in the evening and I was on my own. I went up to have a look at the stars to see if they had an answer. It was as hot as ever.

I lay on my old ancestor's sloping seat beneath his antique telescope and looked up at the stars. Usually the study brought peace and detachment. I saw now that I had always used it as a means of escape—not a bad one, but a real one. But now I could no longer escape. In looking at the stars I was looking at the ultimate reality. The bright patterns I studied with such interest were not standing still, although they appeared so sometimes to me. Instead I was seeing an evolving universe, complete with stars new born and stars dying, showing our world the way from what it once was to what it will one day be. I knew that as I looked at this seemingly changeless night sky I was looking at the birth and death of worlds. The comet, every night brighter, was no true wanderer but was caught forever in an elastic net of forces.

As I was, I thought. No, there was no comfort to be extracted from the stars tonight.

I went down the stairs and got out a bottle of the wine provided for me by Catherine, and sat down to write to her. The wine was a rich red Burgundy and reminded me of her. It helped me to write a long letter to her, telling her everything about Piers. I told her the whole complicated story, ending up with the surprise information from Barbara New at Mallards. Writing it down cleared my mind. I drank another glass of wine, put the letter in an envelope and sealed it, and lolled back on a leather sack to relax.

"Hello."

I looked up. "Simon! You surprised me." He padded round on the stone stairs and thick carpets without making a noise. "I didn't hear you."

He came over and sat down opposite me. "I am a quiet person." He made himself comfortable on a leather pillow. It hadn't really been designed for such a long thin frame as his, so he overlapped at each end. "I'm very cosy down below in my cavern . . . it is a sort of cave, isn't it? I do see the light, though, and I daresay the sun might even penetrate at high noon. Not that I'm around then. Hot, isn't it?"

I held out a glass of wine, and he took it gratefully. "Beaded bubbles winking at the brim, eh." He took a long draft. "Good stuff. Vintage, I suppose."

"I don't believe you know anything about wine," I said skeptically.

"No. Got no palate. But you look the sort of girl who has vintage wine."

"Thank you. I suppose it is a compliment?"

He smiled. "Go along with you, you're always collecting compliments. You should hear what old Montague said when you had gone that night. Made Auntie May almost jealous. Well, it could have done if the stars hadn't told her that your future was, as she put it herself, like a luster glass split in two. Work that one out, if you can." He took another long drink. "Yes, it's made you a sort of cult object to her. She thinks you're going to be a great romantic and tragic figure."

"Well, thanks again," I said.

"It's up to you to prove her wrong. You will, won't you?" He took another long drink. "She says you came with the comet and you'll go with the comet."

"Is she mad?"

He opened his eyes wide. "No. Eccentric, maybe." He held out his glass and I refilled it. "Been working?"

"Just writing a letter."

"I don't do as much of that as I ought. I don't keep in touch with many people."

"Except Grace May."

"Oh, her, of course."

"And Piers."

"Piers came back. Oh God, it's close tonight. Don't you feel it?"

"Yes, it is hot." I had laughed at Grace May and her preoccupation with the stars in their astrological aspects, but in Steeple Minden and especially here in the old observatory it was easy to believe in their influence. Life had been so full of strangeness since I came here that I could almost believe a wind was blowing through the Tarot cards and shaping events.

Simon said, "In holding Piers in my heart, I was holding you. When he came back, you came back, too. We belong together now, Christy. Don't you feel it?"

I was silent; I didn't see myself as a girl who went to Tibet. But I had guessed already that for him Tibet was a dream and not a place.

"You don't answer. Perhaps it's just as well. Keep quiet for now and perhaps one day you can say what I want." He was speaking in a low voice, not looking at me, hardly even seeming to address me. A dream again, I thought.

But because I was touched, because I wanted to return a confidence for a confession, I told him the last turn of the screw. He listened avidly, taking it all in.

"Of course you mustn't go," he said at once.

"I shall go. I'm determined on it."

"You don't know anything about this woman. She might be a madwoman, a criminal even. You don't know what her real motives are in telephoning you and telling you this story. She probably wants to meet you for some purpose of her own. Don't go."

"You make it all sound so sinister," I said, bewildered.

"How silly you were to insert that advertisement." He sounded really angry. "I wish I'd seen it. But I rarely read the papers. I'd have told you what I thought of it as an idea. Asking for trouble. You really are insanely naive. Innocent even."

Suddenly we were quarreling.

"What sort of a person *did* you think you'd get answering?" He was shouting at me.

"She sounded perfectly respectable."

"Respectable!" He almost spat the word at me, he was so angry. "For goodness sake, Christabel. She sounds mad to me."

"Well, not to me, and I spoke to her."

There was a moment of dead silence between us. Simon put out one hand to me pleadingly. I reached out and took it and gave it a squeeze.

"All the same, I *will* go to meet her," I repeated to Simon.

I had no response to my letter to Catherine. It was possible she was abroad. I had no reason for thinking this except that I had begun to feel terribly alone. Not frightened, but solitary. It was a strange feeling, as if I were enclosed in a bubble, with a thin film separating me from the rest of the world.

But I would reach out from my bubble and touch Barbara New.

A restlessness fizzed in my veins after the telephone call from Barbara New. Too many strange things were happening too close together, any one of which, coming alone, could have been reasoned away, but which now clustered too thick for comfort. Above and beyond all else was the mystery of Piers's letter to me. The *apparent* letter from him, I said to myself, urging reason.

The key to Folly House began to loom like a burning symbol in my mind. To what mysteries might it not be the key?

In the heat of the afternoon, the day before I was to meet the woman from Mallards in Brayford, I walked round the lake and then over the hill through the trees to look down on Folly House. Hardly a leaf stirred in the still air. I knew there were animals and birds in the woods, but none moved. The house itself looked dead, with all its doors closed and the blinds drawn against the scorching heat.

Slowly I went toward it. The library windows were tight shut and the blinds closed it in. If I couldn't look in, neither could I be seen. There were always the dogs, though. I had to mind them.

The key felt hot and heavy in my hand.

I wasted a few minutes at the front door, fumbling with the lock; I was opening the door when I saw the postman cycling slowly up the drive. Since it was impossible to ignore him, I waited.

He arrived, mopping his brow. "Terrible hot, isn't it, miss? Building up for a storm." He gave me a smile. I guessed he knew who I was and something of my connections with Folly House. The village gossip was efficient.

I nodded. "It could be."

He squinted at the sky. "Might hold off for today. But it'll come in the end, you'll see." He held out a small pile of letters. "Here's the mail."

I accepted the letters; he got on his cycle and slowly pedaled off, giving me a friendly wave before he disappeared round a bend.

In the hall I put the letters down on an old oak chest. One fell to the ground and I bent to pick it up.

It had fallen address side down, so that I could see the back. On it was a crest printed in red. A bird that looked like a duck, and above it a large M.

Mallards, I thought, he's had a letter from Mallards.

I picked the letter up and put it with the others on the oak chest, tucking it among them so it was hidden.

I had a chill, sinking feeling in the pit of my stomach. So Kit Temple was corresponding with Mallards? I could hear Barbara New's voice saying, "I have a customer near Brayford."

Was this customer Kit Temple?

The door had closed itself quietly behind me, making the hall very dark. There was no sign of life or movement in the house. Neither dogs nor master were making a sound. I could feel my heart beating. Let sleeping dogs lie, I thought, with a slight touch of hysteria.

I was just getting my courage together to search the house, looking for who or what I hardly dared to admit to myself, when a sound made me stop short.

111

I could hear the engine of a motor car. I listened: a car was approaching the house.

I went to one of the small windows that flanked the great door and looked out. A Range-Rover, driven by Kit Temple, swept round the corner and disappeared toward the stables, now garages, at the back of the house. The dogs were with him; I could see their faces pressed against the rear window.

I drew back from the window. So he *did* sometimes leave the house. And, contradicting Simon, he drove.

I didn't want to meet him. I slipped out through the door and fled across the garden and up the hill, effacing myself in the shade of the trees as soon as I could, and hurried back to the old observatory.

In that short trip I had added two more disquieting thoughts to those already assembled in my mind. I would have some sharp questions to put to Barbara New.

Five

——◆▶——

Time seemed to move very slowly as I sat waiting for
Barbara New in the Creamery Coffee Shop. Tommy was
not on duty today, and instead a doll-faced girl stood behind the counter, dispensing tea and coffee with dreamy
efficiency. So far I was her only customer.

"Where's Tommy?" I asked.

"Day off, it is," she said briefly. "More cream for you?"
She pushed a jug of yellow cream toward me.

"No more, thank you." I suppose I had hoped to see
Tommy again. Talking to him, watching his gentle,
shrewd face, would give solidity to an occasion which was
beginning to take on a thin, unreal quality. Perhaps I had
thought of asking his advice. No good now though, he
was not here. I drank my coffee and looked at my watch.

A minute or two yet until the time appointed for our
meeting. I wondered what she was like, this Barbara
New. From her voice I imagined her to be about thirty, or

older, sophisticated and sure of herself. Well dressed, no doubt, and distinctly intellectual of countenance. You had to be all those things to work at Mallards.

I fidgeted around, then carried my coffee from the counter to a seat in the window where I could watch for her. I felt uneasy in my skin.

I thought the unease was physical, as the heat was intense, but mind and body were interacting strongly at the moment.

"Waiting for someone?"

I looked up to find the girl behind the counter staring at me with sympathy.

"Oh yes, I am in fact," I admitted reluctantly. "How did you know?"

"Oh, you've got the look." She shrugged. "I know it. I do a lot of watching and waiting myself."

I looked at the clock on the wall and then checked it with my watch. Both told me the same thing: that my expected visitor was overdue.

I pushed my coffee away, feeling sick. There was beginning to be a hideous similarity between this waiting time and my vigil for Piers.

"Go out and walk around for about half an hour, and when you come back he'll probably be waiting for *you*," she advised.

"Yes." I didn't tell her it was a woman I was awaiting. "I believe I'll do that."

I got up and walked out of the Creamery. Slowly, aimlessly, I wandered through the streets. There were so many reasons why she could be late.

The noonday shadows were black and precise on the pavement. The passers-by were walking slowly, as if the heat was too much for them. There was plenty of traffic, since Friday was market day, but even this moved sluggishly. An exception was an ambulance which appeared briefly at a crossroads ahead of me and then swiftly disappeared, bell ringing. I knew the Brayford hospital was not far away.

I turned and walked back to the Creamery Coffee Shop. A boy was eating ice cream in a corner of the room, and a woman was standing at the counter. She had her back toward me.

I took a deep breath and walked forward. As I approached the counter I saw her push forward some money.

"Here, give me a cup of coffee, quickly, please." The money rattled on the counter, as if she had dropped it in a hurry.

Her voice was the slow, warm voice of a country-woman, not the educated tones of Barbara New. As she turned to stand sideways at the counter I saw a plump, sun-tanned face. But underneath the tan was a pallor, and her hand was shaking.

"I've nearly been run down by a lunatic. I could have been killed. Don't know how I wasn't. Driving like she was mad." The woman seized her coffee cup and drained it. "I could see her at the wheel, her face all distorted. She shouldn't have been allowed to drive. *I* wouldn't have let her."

"What a terrible thing, Mrs. Barton," said the counter girl, her eyes wide. "You look quite shaken up."

"I feel it, Kitty." Her hand trembled as she put the cup back on its saucer; I could hear the china rattle.

"Poor thing."

I licked my dry lips. "Which road was she driving?"

The woman seemed to see me for the first time. "Out toward the Mindens," she said. "An accident looking for somewhere to happen, she was."

I closed the door of the Creamery behind me and walked away, through the town to the Steeple Minden road. The woman driver couldn't be Barbara New, I told myself, but the question stayed in my mind.

I began to walk faster. Soon, almost without knowing when I began, I found I was running.

Then I stopped and took a breath. Why was I running?

I was running because I thought the car with the mad woman driver was my contact, Barbara New.

But how stupid to run, I thought. I could never catch up with her. She must already be miles away. Simon had been right in his assessment of her. She wasn't a stable person. Probably almost everything she had said to me on the telephone had been either a deliberate lie or else a fantasy of her own.

More slowly now I walked on, still following the road to Steeple Minden. I might hitch a lift.

Just outside the town the road wound itself downhill in a sharp decline to where it crossed the river by means of a squat, humpbacked bridge. Something seemed to be happening there.

I looked down. From where I stood I could see that near the bridge there had been an accident involving at least one car. The traffic had been halted, one police car had already arrived, and a second one was just screaming into position, lights flashing. A man got out and ran toward the crashed car; at that moment another figure turned and began to run toward him, arms waving.

Immediately there followed an explosion and then flames appeared, shooting upward with bright fingers. A dark cloud of smoke rose up.

I began to run down the hill. A fire engine passed me, and then an ambulance.

As I ran I was not conscious of any noise. Everything seemed to take place in complete silence. People and vehicles appeared to glide into position as if pulled by outside forces into their inevitable places.

From this curious consequence of shock I was delivered suddenly. I was close to the scene of the accident when, almost with a click, as if a valve had turned, my senses came back and I was bombarded by sounds and smells: shouting and a smell of burning rubber and metal, with the terrible hint of a smell of something much worse scorching to its death.

I stood there watching. The wrecked car was smoldering now, the firemen withdrawing their hose and preparing to retire from the scene. As they went out, the ambulance men moved in.

On the grass a few remnants of personal possessions had survived: a handbag and a bunch of keys. One thing seemed clear, the victim was a woman.

I pushed my way through the crowd to where the policeman stood. "Is it known who she was?" I asked.

He shrugged. "Not that I know of. Not yet. It may take time."

"I think she *may* be a woman called Barbara New. If so, she was coming to meet me in Brayford."

"She was driving *out* of Brayford," he said.

"Yes, I know. I can't explain it."

He turned away, skeptical, indifferent. "I expect you're mistaken, miss. Forget it. Your friend will turn up."

"No," I said, feeling wretched. "No. I'm sure."

I felt fingers grip my arm and turned quickly.

"Christabel." It was Simon. "What are you doing here?"

"I came to see Barbara New. I told you I would. I'm sure that's her in the car. She's dead."

"Come away, Chris." He was drawing me back. "You don't know it's her."

"No. Not yet. It will be, though, you'll find."

"Oh, Christabel." He sounded angry.

117

"She's been killed in an accident, like Piers. Funny, isn't it?"

Gently he eased me through the onlookers, who were leaving anyway, now that the main excitement was over. The ambulance had departed, and there wasn't much left to see except the burned-out shell of a small car.

"I'm going to get you home," he said.

"How do *you* come to be here yourself?"

"Cycled in to Brayford to do some shopping." He pointed to his bicycle propped against a milestone. Six miles to Steeple Minden, the stone said. Seventy-eight to London.

"I want to find out about the woman," I repeated. "I want to know for sure who she was."

"You're as obstinate as an old donkey. I tell you no one will know for sure yet. It may take ages to identify her."

"I don't think so," I said. "I'm going to the hospital." Simon made an irritated noise. "Well, to the police, then."

"Oh, be reasonable, girl."

A car horn hooted at me and I looked round. "Hello there." It was Grace May. "Want a lift back home?"

She was sitting at the wheel of her car, which was a neat little estate car. It matched her: she was a neat little person. She had Dr. Montague with her. Judging by the parcels in the back of the car, they had both been shopping.

"Drive you home?" she repeated. "Terrible business, this accident, isn't it?"

"I think I know who she was." I did not use the present tense: there was no way the woman could be alive. "I want to find out."

"She has this mad idea," said Simon. "Stop her, will you?"

"I want to go to the police station and ask."

"My dear," said Grace, with sympathy, "how could you know her? Not your sister, I hope?" Her eyes were full of interest.

"No. Simply a woman I was going to meet. Don't ask me any more."

"It's all part and parcel of some silly notions she has," said Simon. "Oh, come back to Steeple Minden, Christabel."

But I was watching Grace May's face. A glance, tacit question and answer, passed between her and Dr. Montague. "I'll take you," she said. "It's as well to find out. Set your mind at rest." The words were reassuring; the tone was not.

"Thank you," I said. "Come on, Simon, if you want to."

When we were in the car, she turned to Dr. Montague and I heard her say in a low voice, "I told you how it would be: the stars showed it. Poor girl, poor girl."

She meant me to hear, I think, and because of this I tried not to show that I had done so, but in spite of my control I know I made a little involuntary sound of protest.

"I don't enjoy being cast as a tragic heroine. Especially against my will. Some terrible things have happened. But I am not inclined to blame the stars for them," I said stoutly. "People make events happen. People. People." The toad beneath the harrow knows, I thought. What events had I set in motion by getting in touch with Barbara New?

She shrugged. "I only point the way. But please yourself. No one is obliged to believe. Only the wise listen." She braked smartly. "Here we are at the police station. You go in: we'll all wait."

"I'll come," said Simon, clambering out of the car after me.

Inside we saw a young sergeant who was at first reluc-

119

tant to help us at all. But because I stayed there, pressed up against his desk, obstinately repeating my plea, he made two telephone calls. The first was to his superior and the second, I guessed, to the mortuary of the hospital.

When he had finished on the telephone he turned to me politely and said that no identification had been possible yet. And then he gave himself the lie by adding that, of course, nothing could be said before her next of kin had been told.

"She was called Barbara New, wasn't she? I know that was her name."

He was silent, saying neither yes nor no. But it was enough for me. I knew that it was indeed Barbara New who had been killed.

"And how did it happen? Is that known?" I asked him.

"Probably a sheer accident," he conceded. "Looks as though she just crashed off the road. No other car involved; smashed herself to bits, though." He added quickly, "You all right, miss?"

"Yes, oh yes," I answered. "Just a bit sick." What had I done when I advertised for information about Piers? What second tragedy had I set in motion?

"Sit down for a bit, miss." He took my arm and led me to a chair. Simon was fussing beside me.

"Get her a glass of water," he said.

When it was produced, I sat sipping it. Sometimes thoughts crowd in on the mind. I looked at the policeman. He looked too young to carry much force in this place, but I thought he would listen to me.

"Listen," I said, "appearances may be deceptive. Who will be doing the post mortem? Your usual doctor? Hadows, is he called? Try someone with sharper eyes."

"Come away," said Simon.

"She may have been murdered," I said.

120

"You shouldn't say things like that, miss, not unless you've got good reason. And have you?" The policeman was kind but incredulous.

"She was coming to meet me. It was an important meeting to us both. I think someone stopped her."

"You're upset. I can see that, miss, and I appreciate it. You go away and calm down. Leave everything to us. And if it's any comfort to you, we don't use Dr. Hadows now, he's retired, we have a new expert."

"I hope he's good," I said bitterly.

"Take her away, sir," he said to Simon. "Cup of hot tea and an aspirin, that's what I advise."

Simon took me back to the car. I got in silently, not meeting Miss May's too-knowing gaze.

Simon was very gentle and sweet to me that evening when we were at home in the old observatory. He made me rest and brought me a meal on a tray. He had a practicality about him, as I had noticed before, which belied his sometimes dreamy manner. This time the meal, a simple salad and omelette, was beautifully set out, and although I had professed not to be hungry, it tempted me. There was a slender beaker of iced coffee to go with it, and a rose on the tray.

"The rose is for you," he said. "Never ask me where I got it."

I sat up against a pillow. "I'd guess Folly House."

"Right in one. I nipped over while you were asleep. Did you know you'd had a nap?"

"I know it now," I said drowsily, and yawned.

"Best thing you could do, sleep. You'd had a shock, and that's exhausting." He settled himself on another cushion before me and stretched out his long legs. "Eat away. I've had mine."

The funny thing was that clothed he looked gauche

and clumsy, whereas swimming he had a neatness and elegance of figure. I smiled.

"What are you laughing at, me?" he said, but not aggressively. He seemed peaceful and relaxed.

"Yes, in a way I was." But I didn't amplify the statement. Instead I got on with eating. "I didn't know I was so hungry."

"Had anything to eat today?"

I thought about it. "No." It's weird the way moods can swing, up, down and roundabout. I had gone to sleep puzzled and wretched: now suddenly I was happy. Happier, anyway. I stretched out my toes luxuriously on the thick carpet. I knew what it was that was happening: my body was taking a holiday. It did this sometimes. In spite of any messages of misery my mind was sending, my body obstinately insisted on being happy. When it did this I just had to relax and enjoy it. I laughed.

"First a smile, now a laugh," said Simon. "Good."

"You're not saying much."

He said, "Yes, I am. Inside me."

Silently I turned back to my meal, carefully buttering a biscuit to eat. It seemed safer. We were getting onto fragile ground. Dangerous for Simon, and possibly for me, too.

He saw the situation himself and moved on. "I'm not saying there isn't something puzzling about the accident today," he said, "because I think there is. But I am saying it's nothing to do with you. Even less to do with Piers," he added.

"There has to be an explanation," I said, looking mulish, I suppose.

"And there is one, what I always said it was: she was unbalanced."

"Poor woman," I said slowly. "No, that's too easy an answer. I can't believe it and I'm not sure you believe it yourself." He looked at me sharply. "I can *feel* that you don't believe it yourself. No, I can't accept it, any more than I can accept what Miss May offers. I get a funny feeling when she starts talking to me—as if she was testing me out somehow."

Thoughtfully, he said, "She is the most honest woman in the world."

"And she wants something from me, some response I can't give, I know."

It was as if shock followed by deep sleep had peeled a layer from my perceptions, like skins from an onion, and I saw and felt clearly all sorts of things half sensed before.

"You believe me, don't you?" I asked Simon.

"I always believe you; you're the most convincing person I know," he said. "And for me, you always will be." He took both my hands in both of his, holding them tight. "Look, this is what I want you to do: I want you to pack up and go back to London. Leave the old observatory, and leave this obsession behind you. You're not getting on with your work of setting the place in order, you know you're not."

"I've been sorting out the so-called museum," I said shortly. "There's not as much stuff here as I thought there would be." Nor was it so valuable, a minor disappointment.

"So go home." He was still holding my hands, but in a warm and comfortable way.

"You're nice, Simon, you really are. But no, I'm not going home, as you put it. I don't think I have a home in that sort of way. And if I do, it's certainly not in London." For too long, as I saw now, Piers had been my emotional home. With him, and within my intellectual sanctuary, I had found protection. No wonder I had been a good student: I had needed to be. One home was gone, but I still had the other. "I'll stay here. I take the work seriously. And there's the comet, you see."

He still hung on to my hands: "I'll tell you one thing— Grace May's not so far wrong when she says the comet means trouble." He yawned. "You know, I think it's changed the weather. I've never known it hotter."

He gave my hand a little slap. "I'm never going to give you orders, that wouldn't suit our relationship at all, would it? And anyway, you're not the girl to take them, but I do so wish you'd go away."

"Nowhere to go," I said. "All my sisters are tied up tight in their own affairs and don't want me. As for my father, I won't mention him. No, the old observatory is all I have."

"You have me," said Simon in a low voice. "Always and forever. You always have."

I looked over his shoulder. The room was still suffused with a golden light, which was slowly ebbing as night came on. I loved these long summer evenings. But now the shadows were gathering. Ghosts creep out of these walls, I thought, ghosts of the old astronomer and his girls and all the people who have sheltered here since. They can't be quite gone. They have a sort of half-life here; my very act of remembrance now gives them that much. And then I thought, No, what nonsense.

"What are you thinking about?" asked Simon. "What is it?"

"Nothing."

"You were frightened." He came and sat beside me and put his arms round me and held me tight. "Dearest, dearest Christabel." One hand started to stroke my head, my cheek and my throat. His touch was light and gentle. Instinctively I moved, arching my neck. It was an unconsciously provocative gesture and his response was to put his mouth on mine hard. Without any volition, my lips

124

responded. Inside myself I was saying, Damn, damn, damn, I didn't mean to do this. All the same, I didn't stop. I could hear my heart thudding. Or perhaps it was his. Things were getting a bit mixed up. "Oh, Christabel darling," I heard Simon mutter. He raised his lips from mine and began to cover my eyes and cheeks with soft, feathery kisses.

I pushed myself away. "All right, Simon," I said breathlessly. Then I sat up and smoothed my hair.

"Well, well," he said. "Miss Iceberg's melted."

I couldn't stop his moment of triumph; I wasn't even sure that I wanted to.

He put his arms round me again, but I drew away. "Don't push it, Simon."

He sniffed at his hand. "I smell of you. I've got the scent of you on my hands." He grinned at me. "Gorgeous. They ought to bottle it."

"They have," I said coldly. "It's an expensive toilet water that you buy in a shop in Jermyn Street."

He gave me a last loving squeeze. "You're a luxurious little beast, aren't you? Nothing but the best." He got up and picked up the tray. "I'll take this to the kitchen. I've opened a bottle of the wine that equally luxurious sister of yours gave you. I'll bring a glass up. Lie back and enjoy it." And he went out.

I got up and went to the window. Outside, the trees were limp and heavy in the heat. I took a deep breath; it was needed. I had seriously underestimated Simon. He wasn't going to be someone I could brush aside. Far from it, in fact. My own response to him both startled and shocked me. I was ashamed of it. I belonged to Piers; I *still* belonged to Piers. I crossed my arms and hugged myself like a frightened child.

I heard Simon come up the stairs, enter the room, and stand behind me. I didn't turn round.

"I'm holding a glass in each hand," he said. "I'm not dangerous at all."

I swung round at once. It's disconcerting when someone you thought you had under control does a switch on you.

"Let's go and sit on the steps and look at those stars of yours and drink the wine."

"They're not my stars."

"Oh, go on. You know you own them." He was cheerful, jeering, immensely sure of himself.

The night sky had a purplish glint I had never seen before. Perhaps it was the effect of the comet, now big and low in the sky, with its tails clearly visible. Looking at it, silent and formidable in its splendor, I could see how earlier, unsophisticated peoples had found such comets terrifying. I was a little frightened myself.

"Supposing the comet hit us?" said Simon idly, sipping the ice-cold wine.

"It's only a mass of gas," I answered. "Not as solid as it looks."

"Could start lots of fires, though. The grass and bushes are tinder-dry as it is."

"The comet won't come that close to us. We're safe enough," I assured him.

"I rather like fires," said Simon dreamily. "I think I'm a suppressed arsonist."

We drank the wine without much more conversation. Simon seemed happy to be quiet and I was glad to be. I had a lot to think about. One name after another rolled around in my mind. Piers, I kept thinking about Piers. I was convinced that his death and the terrible death of Barbara New were connected. They must be. I did not believe in coincidences of this nature. Her death had been too opportune. She had been on her way to me, or so I thought, but the evidence suggested that she had been

126

driving around wildly as if in a panic. What was it the woman in the Creamery Coffee Shop had said? I could hear her voice now: "I could see her at the wheel, her face all distorted."

I got up and started to walk around. Simon got up too. "What is it?"

"Just thinking about the woman in the car."

"Why don't you give it a rest?"

I ignored what he said. "She was distressed, very distressed. Something bad must have happened to her even before that accident."

"How do you know?"

"Never mind. I know."

"You've got that closed look on your face."

"I don't really want to talk about it."

He studied my face. "That means you're going to do something."

"Barbara New was going to meet a person she knew, someone who lived near here. She said so to me. I think that person was Kit Temple. At all events, I'm going to try to find out."

"You'd better stop now, Christabel. Please do. I'm sure you're heading for trouble. Danger even. I don't trust that man."

Then something very strange happened: something I find difficult to explain. Simon suddenly said, "What would you do if Piers *did* come back?"

"But he can't."

"How would you choose between him and me?"

"Piers has gone. I believe that now."

"That's not answering. I'd give him back to you, you know, if I could."

"Thank you." It was a mutter from me.

"Oh, no thanks are needed. None earned and none needed."

He took my hand in his and we walked down to stroll by Axwater. It looked deep and dark in the strange starlight, but the woods above it seemed to glint and move with light.

That was strange, but not the strangest thing of all. By the lake—although it was evening, and many of them were quiet, secretive animals which sought seclusion when they slept—crouched many creatures. I saw rabbits, a badger, deer and a vixen. None of them was obvious, but once you saw one you saw the others. They were close to the water as if there alone was safety.

We walked up the path from the lake with arms round waists in a friendly, juvenile way. Or so I thought. Perhaps Simon thought differently.

"What are you going to do then?" he asked.

"About Kit Temple? Haven't made up my mind."

"No. *Not* Kit Temple. About me." As if to emphasize his question, he pulled me closer to him.

For a moment I yielded, then something caught my eye and I moved away. Simon made an irritated noise and tried to pull me gently back. "No, wait, Simon. Look, what's that? I can see a light. And another. There, on the path from Steeple Minden." I was pointing.

A chain of lights could be seen, as if a procession of people, each carrying a small lamp, was approaching.

I turned to him. "Simon, what is it?"

"I don't know." But I got the impression he did know and was angry.

"I'm going to look." I was already running forward.

I had not far to go before the leader of the walkers hailed me. "Hallo there. Greetings." It was the unmistakable voice of Grace May. I was half surprised and half oddly satisfied inside, as if I'd always known she'd turn up here. Alba Bailey had alerted me to the possibility of a

128

visit. "Ask me," I had said, but of course Grace May had chosen her own time. After all, she had the stars to advise her, didn't she?

I stood there waiting for her to come up to me. Unconsciously I had taken up a formal, posed stance at the top of the rising path, like a priestess waiting for her worshippers. The thought came to me quickly as the file of people, about six in all, drew close. Miss May led the line and Dr. Montague came next, and I recognized the girl from the library in Brayford among the rest. What I said was coldly secular: "What is all this?"

"Bless you, my dear." She sounded as if she really was offering me a benediction. "May we all come up? Oh, thank you, child, thank you." She was breathless but never ceased to talk. "Come along, those people behind. Be careful where you tread. Walk delicately now." She looked up at me, answering the question I had not expressed. "One always walks delicately on holy ground."

"*Is* this holy ground?"

"Oh yes. Axwater and this hill." She nodded her head with conviction. "Axwater and the hill have a long history behind them as a holy place. I dare say that is what drew your revered ancestor to build the observatory here."

"He was drawn by the geography of the land." I know my voice was harsh.

"It's the same thing." Her voice was correspondingly gentle. "It was because of its geography, the unique relationship between hill, sky and water, that the ancients found it holy." She added prosaically, "And in any case, in my experience holy ground is usually rough ground, so it is sensible to watch where you put your feet. Some of us aren't as young as we were."

The rest of the walkers had caught up with her now. Dr. Montague, the girl from the library, a middle-aged

129

woman, an older man, a boy in his teens, and two elderly women who stood together and looked like sisters.

"*Now* you're wondering who we are, aren't you?" said Grace May, with that maddening touch of telepathy she often displayed.

"No." I could play that trick, too, only I called it intelligent guessing. "You're the Brayford and Steeple Minden Discussion Group. I recognize one of your members." The librarian blushed. "Only what you are doing here, I don't know."

"We had met in my house by arrangement for a talk by me on the Tarot cards," said Grace May. "But the cards would not behave for me."

She spoke with utter conviction as if she really meant it. "Try as I would, I could not even lay them out." She stretched out her fingers. "They were like boards—rigid, unmoving. Finally I knew what it was. This has happened to me once before. It indicates a change to where the forces are more favorable."

I could see the librarian's eyes shining; Alba Bailey was loving every minute of it. Dr. Montague shuffled his feet.

"Come along now, Grace, tell her what you want."

"We want to come inside, lady of the tower. The solution *before* was to read the Tarot pack on the floor of the old observatory."

I hesitated. "It's late."

"Now is the time," she said with complete assurance. "I should like to lay out the Tarot pack here tonight." She put one hand like a plump little paw on my arm. "You don't like the idea, do you?"

"No."

"I assure you that no harm can come to you."

"I wasn't thinking of that."

"Weren't you? But I was." She truly was like a sleek,

130

bright-eyed cat, gentle now, but with paws of sheathed menace.

I swallowed my reluctance. "Come on, then. I don't know about the floor, though. This place is all covered with thick carpet."

"Even on the very top floor, where the telescope is?"

"No, not there."

"That is where I wish to be."

She led the way forward without hesitation. I caught at her hand. "Wait . . . have you been here before? Have you held meetings like this in the tower often before?"

Her eyes were veiled at once. "Yes," she admitted. "It was occasionally a place I came to. How could it be otherwise?"

How I must have got in her way, I thought, just by being here. Before my brother-in-law redecorated the tower, and before I came, the place must have been wide open to her to use as she wished. She could have held a whole witches' coven here and no one would have known. She looked at me and smiled blandly. "Forward, then," she said.

Silently I trudged up the stairs behind them all. Simon followed me.

"Why don't you get rid of her?" he whispered. He sounded angry.

"Can't," I whispered back. And it was true, I knew I couldn't have stopped her.

"Oh, Christabel!"

"Hush, she'll hear." Grace May had turned and given us a glance; I thought she had heard us already.

As I went into the room she said to me, "In fact you are not so averse to our being here now, are you?"

I didn't answer, but of course she was right. The arrival of Grace May and the rest had put a barrier between

131

Simon and me at a moment when I was glad enough to have it there. I wasn't sure what would have happened between us at that moment if they had not arrived. With that quick intuition of hers, she had sensed it. If I'd challenged her I expect she would have given the stars the credit.

"Oh, my dear friend," she said to Dr. Montague, "find the switch and put one light on, just one. Ah, splendid. Now all gather round. Friends to the right, enemies to the left, for left is the sinister side."

Not unnaturally, no one went to the left. Simon and I were already standing there, so we stayed in our sinister isolation.

Grace May dropped to her knees, popping on a pair of horn-rimmed spectacles as she did so, thus changing her appearance from pussy cat to owl. "Now you mustn't interpret my position as one of prayer or supplication. No, it is expedience only. The floor gives me more room to lay out the cards." I had known other schoolteachers with that jokey manner. It didn't mean they had a sense of humor. "And I believe you're short of tables here," she continued, giving me an upward glance.

"You believe right," I said.

"With you, I usually am," she said comfortably. "There is a flow between us, I find." She was placing her cards on the floor as she spoke. "Cut, my dear, if you will."

I knelt beside her and cut the cards. She smiled. "The nine-card spread will meet our needs tonight, I think, because we are seeking instruction. Instruction." She repeated the word with satisfaction, as if it came pleasantly to her. "Had we, now, wished to pose a specific question, I would have suggested the seven-card spread." She put her head on one side. "And then I have a special little layout of my own for the really important question." She

132

directed her gaze to what I could only think of as her class. "But all that will come later." Alba Bailey gave a little squeak of anticipation.

She had the cards face down on the floor in front of her in four irregular lines. A card lifted in the breeze that suddenly moved in the room; I saw her look up quickly. She straightened the card, which had fallen back crooked.

Quite clearly I could see The Fool in his bright archaic dress and belled cap. Next to The Fool was The Hermit, holding up his lamp to look into the dark. It was The Hermit that had moved and I now saw that his card had fallen across The Wheel of Fortune, which seemed to be spinning. I blinked my eyes and the wheel steadied.

The wind lifted another card, and I heard her make a little murmuring sound under her breath. It sounded as if she said, "What strength." Although I couldn't be sure that was what she said, I know it was at me she looked. A wave of irritation moved inside me. The card that had moved was The Empress.

"Stay still, dear," she said.

"I am still."

"In the body, perhaps."

I took a deep breath and tried to relax.

"Oh, thank you," she said at once.

She was kneeling on the floor. The rest of the group was standing quietly, staring down at what she was doing. The women of the party had expressions of calm interest, but the man and the boy seemed self-conscious. In fact the boy looked as if he would like to depart rapidly, but the middle-aged woman had a firm grip on his arm. There seemed a link among the three: I guessed they were a family.

The cards were in the light; the rest of the room was shadowy. The old telescope on its platform took up the center of the room. I could see the mass of it out of the corner of my eye. Seen in this light, it looked at once bigger and less substantial than usual.

The edges of the room blurred and my attention became focused on the cards, shining with light. Grace May was talking, but her voice seemed distant. I wondered what was the true purpose of this expedition here tonight. Something more than she had told, I was sure. I didn't trust her, or even like her. She seemed constantly to tremble on the edge of saying something profound, but it was never said, and for my money it never would be. I suppose what I was expressing to myself was my belief that she was a sham and a poseur, laying claim to powers and techniques she did not possess. She had something, though, a sensitivity and a quickness of mind that I was forced to acknowledge, and this gave her power of a sort. I suppose I'd got in her way, arriving to stay here at the observatory. The place seemed important to her.

The cards seemed to be getting bigger and bigger, dazzling my eyes. My eyes watered and I blinked. The cards shrank to normal size.

I could hear Grace saying, "Since we have no specific questions to ask, but have simply come to learn what the cards have to tell us, I will turn the cards one after the other, beginning on the left." She stretched out a delicate hand toward the cards. "Another point: always turn the card itself from left to right. In that way you do not disturb its position if it should be upside down."

A wind was calling gently outside the walls of the old observatory. Then it seemed to get into the room and move around among us like another presence. I don't think I was the only person to notice because I saw Alba Bailey shiver, and the boy, of all people, rubbed his hands together as if he were cold.

Carefully, slowly, Grace was turning the cards. She

134

would turn her eyes from the card to the onlookers as if she was really instructing them. Yet all the time I had the feeling it was a charade, and that the person she was really instructing was me. But to what purpose?

"Ah, first we have The Lion. Yes, and upside down too. If upright, ladies and gentlemen . . ." Here she gave a quick look at Simon, who scowled back: he hadn't spoken the whole time. "If upright, The Lion signifies strength, but upside down, well, that's different. Do not lose your courage, we might interpret it as saying: An ordeal is coming, but face it. And there is another implication: physical danger is involved. Yes, the danger is real. . . . There is an *animal* element. Never forget that." She sat back on her heels. "So there we have a warning of danger for someone in this room."

"Perhaps for all of us," suggested one of the women a little nervously.

"Let me turn another card. Ah yes, here we have The Lady. Upside down again, so she pairs with the other card. Danger, troubles." She shook her head, moving quickly on to another card.

I saw a picture of a chariot drawn by winged beasts whipped on by a crowned, standing figure.

"The Chariot," she said swiftly. "You see The Chariot? It always means movement and action. It was one of the cards that moved. Did you notice that? Someone is trying to get back."

The room was becoming very dark and hot. But even in the heat one could feel touches of cold. It was as if the room were striped with bands of cold and heat that rotated over us as if we were on a wheel. The Tarot Wheel, I thought, The Wheel of Fortune. Then I thought, Oh, rubbish—only to hear a low moan from someone among the others in the room.

A rumble of thunder crept in from outside. Then there

135

was a flicker of lightning, making the lamplight dim, then another grumble of thunder. The librarian, Alba Bailey, moved round to stand near me: she and Grace exchanged a look.

Grace May turned over one more card. "Ah, The Magician. The Magician has come. Yes, he's joined us."

There was a high scream. I spun round. I thought it might be Alba, but she was standing silently behind me, although her eyes met mine in a frightened way. The scream had come from the boy. He was crouching on the floor pointing with one forefinger outstretched. "Look, he's there; he's there in the chair! The Magician. The old astronomer."

I looked at the chair slung beneath the telescope. It was just possible to believe that a faint, shadowy figure was resting there.

I snapped on a second lamp and then another; the room filled with light. Of course there was nothing in the chair, no ghostly shape, no old astronomer. I didn't know how I could have thought there was even for a moment. I had to hand it to Grace May. She had worked us all up finely. Now she was crouched there on the floor by the cards, looking old and tired in the harsh light. Yes, and frightened; she looked frightened. Slowly she stood up. "Over for the time being," she said.

The party broke up soon after that, its members murmuring words of thanks or apologies according to their moods. The boy still looked distraught, but he too apologized. More than once, in a shy, shamed voice.

"What did you make of all that?" Simon closed the door behind them.

"I don't know, but whatever it was, it wasn't just a little lesson in how to use the Tarot pack. Grace May was trying to say something. To me, probably. If not, then to you."

136

"No. Not me."

"No, it wouldn't be. I suppose I'm The Lady. And someone is coming, and there is danger. It's not the first time she's said that sort of thing, is it? And what does it all amount to? If you're cryptic enough, and vague enough, you can always produce something that comes true. In the course of nature people arrive and very often there is danger. And this talk of 'animals': we're all animals, aren't we? You, me and Grace May."

"That's quite a speech." He was looking up at me from the bottom of the flight of stairs. His face, foreshortened by the distance, looked young and tired.

"Over now." I yawned and waved a hand to him. "Good night."

Slowly I walked up the stairs to my own room. Bed was a welcome thought.

There was no doubt in my mind that Grace May had contrived this evening's entertainment for reasons of her own. But I had a funny feeling that she had got more than she bargained for.

At the end she had looked frightened. Alba Bailey had also appeared scared. The other participants had seemed embarrassed or interested, according to their natures. Even the boy who had cried out had acted self-conscious as he left, but not as if he were afraid. Only those two women had shown fear of what had been conjured up.

I myself was not afraid (although I had been given a strong hint by Grace May, working through the cards, that I *should* be), but I would have been glad to know what I had really seen in the old astronomer's chair.

When Alba had pressed my hand in goodbye she had whispered, "Don't worry, there was nothing really there in the chair," and I had answered, "Oh, but there was, because I saw it."

As I lay in bed, I wondered why I had said what I did to

137

Alba. I didn't quite believe it myself. I think I said it to frighten Alba, and in this I had handsomely succeeded. But she had been frightened before. I could have sworn that I had detected a look of horrified collusion passing between her and Grace May as the boy screamed. Was I imagining it? In my present mood it was so easy to imagine so much.

I tossed and turned, unable to sleep, my mind full of questions that were hard to formulate and even harder to answer. In these dark hours of the night I was in the mood to doubt everybody, including myself.

After a while I sat up, propped a pillow behind me, and stared into the darkness. I found the courage then to admit what I hadn't wanted to face before: that a good deal of my present distress and confusion was because of the way I had responded to Simon.

I was even a little frightened by the way my body had leapt to life. What had happened to clever, cool Christabel Warwick, who was always in control of the situation? Temporarily not at home, I told myself ruefully, and I hoped her absence *was* only temporary.

I had loved Piers for so long that it was hard to admit now that my love, my innocent, adolescent love, was over. But this was the admission I had to face. I was a woman now with a new sort of love to offer, and it had taken Simon to show me. I felt shy and a little awkward about it all, which was silly, because I was a grown person and no more innocent than the next. In theory, anyway.

I sat staring into that hot and dark night. I knew I was saying goodbye to Piers. But I had to lay his ghost and give it rest. "What are you going to do?" Simon had asked. "I don't know," I had answered, talking about Kit Temple. But I had lied: I had known what I meant to do. I meant to search Folly House.

Murder is a secret event, but it also cries out with a loud voice. If Kit Temple had killed Piers and the woman from Mallards, Barbara New, then there would be some traces, some evidence somewhere in his house, and in his way of life. Indeed, in his face and manner I thought I could see such signs already. Kit Temple himself might be quite unaware of the spoor he had left, but I, the hunter, would know it when I saw it.

I would search Folly House from top to bottom. After all, he had given me a key to the house, had he not? I had sought and sought in my mind for the real reason he had handed over the key (I had never quite accepted that it was for *my* convenience) and had never come up with anything. Now I wondered if he was not asking, as they say the guilty so often ask, to be found out.

I felt sick as I put that question to myself, and the sensation of sickness surprised me. But like someone who suspects a fatal illness and so is too fearful to examine her symptoms, I did not look closely into my despair.

Six

In the morning Simon was gone before I got up, leaving a note to say he was off on various bits of business of his own. Tactful of him to absent himself, I thought; he had an instinct not to obtrude. I knew that he had his letters sent care of Grace May at her cottage, and I guessed he had probably gone to collect them. He wasn't very regular about it, as if nothing urgent could ever await him there. Lately he had hardly spoken of his Himalayan enterprise. At first he had been full of it, mentioning people who might go with him and naming the distinguished scientific institutions that had promised support, but during the last few days the prospect seemed to have receded further into the future. I hoped I had had nothing to do with it. I wondered how he managed about money, but I guessed that there was a small private income behind him somewhere. He never seemed to lack for money, but neither did he have a regular job, and he had to live somehow.

The time for the postman's delivery had come and gone by the time I had dressed and made some coffee. I had attired myself carefully in a blue denim skirt and an old silk shirt. My hair, which I usually wore loose, I now pinned up high on my head. It wasn't until I was all ready that I realized I had unconsciously got myself up in the clothes I always used for dirty or unpleasant tasks. Even my hair was pinned because I had an unwanted picture of strands of it catching in something or being held in clutching hands. In my pocket I put a small torch and some matches; I had great difficulty in preventing myself from adding a block of chocolate. I don't like chocolate much, but it's good nourishment and keeps you going for a long time (so Simon said). Back for lunch, I said to myself, and slid the chocolate into a drawer.

I told myself it was still too soon to expect an answer to my letter to Catherine, that I even didn't mind if the postman hadn't brought anything for me, but the truth was that I *did* mind. I wanted to hear Catherine's voice speaking to me; I needed to hear her clear decided tones, uttering good sense; but above all, I wanted to hear that voice, so like my own, giving me its unspoken assurance that the blood tie still held and that I was not alone. There are times when you need your own reality established: Catherine could always do that for me. And without trying, just by being herself, because part of her was the same as part of me: our genes matched.

On an impulse, I picked up the telephone and dialed her number. I'm usually tough with impulses of this sort where Catherine is concerned. Because I value our relationship, because she really has been more to me than any sister usually is, I tried not to make too much of it, not to hang on to her in any way. Lovely ladies like Catherine don't want little sisters hanging around.

The telephone rang and rang; I thought at first there wasn't going to be any response. Then a man's voice answered. "Hello?"

Oh. Oh, well, I thought, and said, "Can I speak to Catherine, please?"

There was a long pause, and then he said, "She's out. Gone to work."

"Oh, is she at her boutique? I could ring there."

"I wouldn't advise it. Who is this speaking?"

"I'm Christabel."

"Are you the little sister? You're giving her a lot of trouble, aren't you?" His voice was cool.

"No," I said. I was surprised. "No, I'm not."

"I think you are. She's had a letter from you and she's done nothing but cry ever since."

"I don't believe it."

"You did write her a letter?"

"I did, yes."

"You can believe it, then."

"Who are you?" I asked. "Not a pop star, are you? Not Peterborough?"

"I'm Ned." He said no more. I suppose, really, there was no need. He was plainly living there.

"But Catherine doesn't cry." I remained incredulous.

"When I say cry," said Ned, "I mean she's been in a bloody foul mood. I mean shout, snarl and brood. It's her way of crying."

"I don't think it's anything to do with me," I said slowly. "I'll ring Catherine at the shop."

I did ring the shop, but no one answered. After a while I gave up and went out into the sunlight. Another little mystery, in a world that was presenting me with too many at the moment. Damn Catherine.

There was some freshness in the air this morning, in spite of the residue of yesterday's heat. I walked down toward Axwater, meaning to take the path through the woods and over the hill toward Folly House.

Simon was by the lake. I could see him sitting there on the ground, hunched up, looking down into the water. He had his back to me.

I don't think he heard my approach on the soft turf, because he looked up with surprise when he saw me.

"Hello." I said. "I didn't expect to see you here. I guessed perhaps you'd gone off to Brayford or Steeple Minden."

"Thought you'd like to be on your own for a bit. I'm just sitting here thinking."

"Oh." I could see my reflection in the clear water; with day all the animals had gone. I couldn't even see a fish swimming.

"About you, if you want to know." He gave me a wry look. "You take some thinking about." Then he added, rather grudgingly, as if he didn't want to tell me but knew he must, "There was a bit on the local radio news about the car crash yesterday. Seems longer ago than yesterday, doesn't it? The report named the woman. Didn't say anything about Mallards, but called her Barbara Mary New from Kensington. So you were right there. A fatal accident, they called it. He paused and looked into Axwater, as if now he did not like what he saw. "The police are asking for witnesses of what happened. There aren't any, of course."

"I could tell them of what the woman in the Creamery Coffee Shop said: about seeing Barbara New driving through the town looking as if she had a demon with her."

"What a horrid vivid phrase," he said lightly. "Yes, I
143

thought you might want to do that. But I should keep out of it, if I were you. After all, it's only hearsay."

But I had been thinking. "I daresay I could find the woman: she was known in the Creamery Coffee Shop."

"Was she now?" He stood up. "Well, I'll take care of that for you if you like."

"Oh, would you? Thank you, Simon. I'm off to Folly House."

"Yes, I'd thought that too." He sounded grim.

"I'm going over that place with a fine-tooth comb," I said, and I could hear my voice sounding gay and determined. Especially the latter.

We were standing face to face now. "I can't persuade you to give up the idea?" Simon asked. He took my hands and swung them gently in his. "It's not the sort of thing you ought to do, do you know that?"

"I don't think good manners comes into it."

"I'm not thinking of good manners," he said sharply, "but of danger. Don't you think you might be in danger?"

This was the day when for the first time the comet was visible in daylight. It hung there in the bright blue sky like a pale ghost of itself, which would gain strength with every passing hour.

I let the word "danger" rest on the hot air. Then I said, "Yes, I believe there will be some danger. I accept that risk."

"Oh, my love, my love," he muttered.

"Don't call me that, Simon, please don't." It took an effort to keep my voice level.

"Do you love me at all? Do you care at all what happens to me? Would you miss me if I wasn't there?"

"Yes, to all those things, but you still mustn't love me. Not yet."

"Oh, you're so cool, cool. I could break up that coolness if I wanted."

144

"Yes," I said. "I think you probably could. But it wouldn't solve anything. Until I've cleared up this business I am still Piers's." It wasn't really true any longer, but I made myself say it.

"That's madness," Simon's voice had an edge on it. "I beg you not to go to Folly House. Break out of this madness. Piers is dead. You can't bring him back and you can't turn yourself into an avenger. I've told you that before, and I tell you again. You will only harm yourself with bitterness and anger. That is the *real* danger to you." There was a ring of real conviction in his voice. I couldn't doubt that he believed every word of what he was saying.

"I want to know," I said doggedly, and when it came to it, a lot of my motive was the plain desire to know. "You take it all too quietly, Simon. But then, it's not happening to you."

"Isn't it?" he said. Then he gave a little laugh, and stopping to pick up a stone from the ground, threw it far, far into Axwater. "Oh, go on. You'd better go if you mean to. I've said all I can say to stop you . . . I could do it by force, I suppose." He looked at me thoughtfully and took a step forward.

I stood my ground. "You'd have to lock me up in the tower," I said defiantly.

"I might do that."

We eyed each other, and his eyes fell before mine, as I knew they must, because my determination was harder. I had won, but all the same I wish we hadn't had this confrontation, because it had unleashed a force, a physical energy inside Simon that crackled between us.

"I'll be gone all day," he said.

"See you this evening."

"Probably."

He swung off down the path to Steeple Minden and I

145

turned to climb through the woods. Before I disappeared among the trees I turned back to wave, but he was striding forward, not looking behind him.

The woods seemed full of secret life this morning. Behind every bush, in every thicket, hiding in every full-leaved branch, I sensed tiny scratchings, stretchings and flutterings.

I could not be in the woods without my mind turning to Piers. I sat down to think about him. Was he dead? After all, was he really dead? The question kept coming back, however much I pushed it aside. There was the strange letter, purporting to be from him. Supposing he wasn't dead but in hiding. Or imprisoned somewhere. My thoughts ran wildly on. What was it the cards had said last night: that someone was coming? I didn't believe in anything the Tarot cards said. I rejected it forcibly, but still I couldn't help hearing the message.

A movement in the woods caught my eye and I stood up. There was someone there.

Ahead of me, where the path dipped into a natural hollow, I saw a small figure. A woman wearing a dark-green, full-skirted dress was kneeling on the grass, feeding a bird. Other birds were on the ground and in the air near her. She had a basket by her side, and from it she was taking what must have been handfuls of food and scattering them around. She was intent on her task, coaxing the bird, which strutted toward her with tail stretched out and neck arched, a delicate and pretty creature.

As I came up, the birds took fright and fled. The woman turned round in annoyance. Of course it was Grace May.

"Oh, it's you." She indicated the bird. "Now you've sent him away. And it's taken me weeks to get him so tame."

"Yes, I saw you feeding a pheasant."

"Oh, I always feed them. You have to. But that one's a friend."

"They're fed now, to be shot later," I observed.

"Oh, no one shoots them here," she said easily. "No one *comes* here much except me."

"I was surprised to see you."

"Oh no, I come often." She looked about her with pleasure. "I come to see the birds and some of the animals, and to gather berries and wild herbs in due season."

The pheasant was already coquetting at her from the shelter of a bush. She made a chirruping noise to it and slowly it advanced toward her. Here in the woods she seemed more natural, less contrived, than when talking about astrology and horoscopes.

"I know every part of these woods," she said. "I've come here since I was a child. I was born the other side of that hill in a woodman's cottage and my grandfather was butler when the old family had it."

"I used to know the woods, too," I said. "Not here—I didn't realize Folly House existed in those days—but I used to walk on the other side of Axwater."

"Yes, I know." She didn't say what it was she knew. "Not changed much, has it? Except for the better."

"For the better?" I didn't know what she meant.

"Not long after you knew it." And here she gave me a fleeting smile, letting me know she had understood when it was that I had been here and had learned to love the woods: when I loved love. She went on, "There was a fire, the woods burned all one night. It's a mystery how the fire started, a tramp perhaps, or so the police thought. I came here myself with all the men from the village, but it was no good. In the end the fire more or less burned itself out. All this part was left charred and black. Folly House was empty then, gathering dust and dry rot."

"Was anyone hurt in the fire?"

She paused. "Have you seen a man working in the woods?"

I nodded. "I have seen someone."

"That's old Joss. He had a bad experience when the woods burned. He was caught between two curtains of fire."

"He escaped though?"

"Oh yes. He did. Kit Temple got him out himself. But Joss had his little granddaughter with him—Mary. She was a mongoloid. She was nearly always with him. She loved the woods. A sweet child, very friendly and gentle. He was carrying her in his arms. But she was dead."

I waited for her to say it was a blessed release, or it was just as well really, as people so often do about unfortunates like Mary, but she didn't.

She went on. "She wasn't touched, but the doctors said her heart just stopped beating through fear. She'd always hated fire, you see."

"What a terrible story."

"Yes. It did something to Joss, broke his mind. You can see it in his face."

"Yes," I agreed. "It does show."

"Kit Temple's been very good to him. Kept him on. Paid him even when he's been hard up himself."

Looking about me, I found it hard to believe that this lush, profuse greenery could so quickly have covered the site of the fire. "How soon it's all grown back," I said.

She smiled. "Ah, but it had help. Kit Temple bought Folly House, and he not only restored the house, he replanted the woodlands too. It wasn't hard, nature had already started the work, but he carried it on. The animals and birds came back on their own, of course. Some of them had never left; there have been foxes and badgers here since time immemorial, and even the fire didn't

148

drive them away, but they were beleaguered. Yes, we owe a lot to what Kit Temple did. He brought the deer back, added White Park cattle—pretty, aren't they? You won't find many in the village to say a word against him, he's a man who loves the land." And yet there was a strange note in her voice.

I looked at her warily: she was telling me something. All the same, you don't like Kit Temple, I thought.

"And he is part owner of the mill in the village, he helped rebuild that too. You've noticed it, I expect?" I shook my head silently. "Small, of course, employs about forty people; but the tweed they weave sells very well and the place itself is quite a tourist attraction. It all brings money to the village and we were dying quietly before that, losing population every year. Now we are growing again. Too much so for my taste—too many things are being changed—but I am alone in this. You won't find Kit Temple has critics in this place."

Once again she had read my mind and sensed my thoughts about Kit Temple.

"Are you warning me?" I asked bluntly.

"Why should I warn you and about what?" she returned blandly.

"Not to expect help in any quarrel with Kit Temple."

"Oh no, no. There is no need. You will not quarrel with Kit Temple. You can't."

I felt like hitting her. "I wouldn't count on it," I said.

"It's not in the cards," she said. "In any case, I've tried to fight him and failed. He gets his way."

Deliberately, I said, "I hate all this talk of what will happen and what will not happen."

"Naturally." She was cool. "It's unwelcome and disconcerting not to feel a free agent."

"I'm on my way down there now to have it out with Kit Temple," I said. "After I've had a good look around."

149

"Are you? Really?" she said. "By the way, I'm sorry about last night. We were something of a disturbance, I'm afraid. Did you sleep well?"

"No," I said. As if she didn't know.

She gave me an oblique look. "Did you notice the old astronomer in his chair? Just for a moment?"

"No," I said at once. "I saw nothing at all."

"Funny, I thought you did. The lad saw him. Surprised me for a bit. Didn't expect anything to happen last night. Not in that way. But there, you never can tell what will come about when you strike certain notes. Are you sure you didn't see anything, not even just a shadow?"

"Quite sure," I said. "A keen lot, aren't they, that discussion group? Quite late for them to turn out and walk through the fields."

"Oh, they loved it."

"So I saw."

She smiled. "Oh, you see and you see, but only occassionally do you admit to it. One remarkable thing, though—" and she paused, waiting to be sure I was listening. "The boy who *also* saw only comes because his mother is afraid to walk home in the dark. He has no interest in the cards or the crystal, yet he sees and she does not." Appraisingly, she said, "Now that shows the nature of the machine, I think."

"Which is?"

She gave a wry smile. "Unfair and unpredictable. Probably unstable as well."

I leaned forward so that I could see right into her eyes. They were shallow and round, reflecting the light like Axwater. "If I asked you to tell me about Piers, whether he is alive or dead, whether he waits for me or has already passed far beyond me, what would you say?"

"I should deal the cards in Saint Andrew's cross and then I should draw the seventh card and then the ninth

150

and then the eleventh and then the thirteenth, and the thirteenth, read with the rest, would give the answer," she said simply. "Only I would expect to draw the Man with the Scythe, otherwise the Hanged Man. Death or disaster, in other words."

"I see," I said. "Thank you."

I suppose I couldn't have expected her to leave it there, and she didn't.

"But in return I might want to ask you why you think Piers could be alive," she said.

Reluctantly, I said, "I had a letter—it seemed to be in his writing—telling me that he had waited for me but I hadn't come. As if he were still alive." I ran over the possibilities. "I suppose it is a forgery. Or if Piers wrote it, then he wrote it years ago in relation to some earlier incident that I've forgotten, and for some reason the letter stayed around and someone sent it to me. As a kind of joke."

"And do you believe that?"

"I don't know what to believe."

"And what would you do if Piers were alive and did return?"

I shook my head to clear it. "I believe I'd explode. That's what happens in the skies, you know, when two bodies meet unexpectedly. I'd just blow up."

"And if he is not alive and still returns?"

"Oh no, no. I don't accept that."

"But, as you know, that makes no difference." There was a sort of iron determination about her that nothing seemed to shake. "If he comes, then it will be to the old observatory or to the woods. They call them the walking woods, did you know that?"

I wanted to cry out and make a protest in the name of rationality and logic and science and all the things that had shaped my life. What she said sounded like a fall back to unreason and the Dark Ages. But I didn't make a noise. Some force about her kept me quiet.

She held out her hand. "Let me help you."

I don't want your help. I'll do things my way, I said, and turned to run away. I said it to myself, only I expect she heard.

I ran deeper into the woods, off the path, losing myself in a tangle of bushes and young trees. Eventually I stopped, drawing in my breath in long deep shudders. I leaned against a tree, resting my cheek against the rough bark and drawing comfort from it. A wild convolvulus trailed its leaves and white trumpets across my face. I moved back and saw that a squirrel had disturbed the creeper. The squirrel shot off up the tree.

I stood there silently trying to pull myself together.

For a few minutes I felt as though I could not go on to Folly House and Kit Temple. I stayed in my enclosure, hiding my face and trying not to tremble.

Then I thought, Perhaps that's what she wanted to achieve—she wanted to stop you.

So I tidied my hair and patted my eyes dry with my handkerchief. Had I been crying? How had I been crying? I hadn't realized, but my cheeks had been wet and my eyes drowned in tears.

I fought my way back onto the path and turned downward toward Folly House.

The weather had changed while I was in my hiding place. The quality of the light had altered.

The bright body that burned in the sky seemed to be summoning up a mist. As I came out of the woods and looked down on the rose garden of Folly House, I saw that the blue of the sky was turning gray and that the comet and the sun were disappearing behind a creeping

152

mildew. By the time I got down to the house a nasty, hard, shadowless light pervaded everywhere.

It made Folly House look painted and shallow, like a child's toy house of cardboard. But as I got closer I saw certain changes. All the windows on the ground floor were open and the heavy curtains were drawn back. Some windows I had never seen unshuttered before were now naked to the light. As I came nearer still, I saw that someone—it had to be a man's hand—had plucked some crimson roses and crammed them into a silver jug and placed them on the windowsill. They looked freshly picked.

The big front door stood open, and as I walked in, one of the little white dogs wandered out to greet me. The trio had long ago ceased to bark at me, although they were still capable of letting out a gentle growl when I left.

Another dog wandered out of the library and then the third. I knew their master could not be far away. Then his voice called to me.

"Hello, I'm in here."

I walked slowly into the library. Music was coming softly from a record player on the table. He was leaning against some cushions on the big leather sofa, a pile of books on a table beside him, a pad of paper on his lap. He looked thinner and paler, but his eyes were bright and his expression cheerful, as if he had met some crisis in his life and successfully passed it.

"Ah, so you're back."

"It has been some time," I admitted.

"Not so long in days, but in other ways—" he looked away from me and out the window "—a long time has passed."

"You look ghastly. Physically." Not mentally or emotionally, though, I thought. Something good has happened to you. It's as if you had had a blood transfusion.

153

"I've been through a black hole and back again. At least that's what it felt like," he said, but cheerfully.

"I'm sorry," I said, formally, stiffly. I suspected him of murder, and he laid claim to having fallen through a hole in the universe.

"Oh, don't be. I think I went through it some time ago, and the method of my re-entry was uncomfortable but effective." He clicked his fingers at the dogs. "You don't know what I'm talking about, do you? But why should you?" The dogs had leapt onto the sofa with him, disposing themselves on his legs.

"I'll tell you what it has been. You have a right to know, I think. I learned yesterday that my nephew Piers did not after all, as I had always believed, steal a very valuable object from this house and then kill himself because he feared what I would do. I had written him a letter threatening him. That was the letter from me which distressed him. Now I know that he stole nothing, and curiously, everything is lightened. Because I had already been instrumental in killing his parents, since it was my wretched car they were driving when they crashed."

"No, Piers did not kill himself," I said. "But I never thought he did." I had to swallow to keep back those tears that seemed so ready to begin again. "But who told you, who helped you to believe what you never should have believed, that Piers was a thief?"

He winced. "Yes, I asked for that. Well, a woman told me, a rather silly woman, I suspect. A woman who worked in the showrooms in London where it was sold. She wrote me a letter."

Mallards and Barbara New seemed to weave themselves into the story in a way I could not account for but knew to be crucial. I thought I had invented her, summoned her up with my advertisement. Now I knew this

154

wasn't true. She had been there all the time, waiting in the wings to make her fatal entry.

"We arranged to meet in Brayford yesterday to talk it over. I had questions to ask. But she didn't turn up."

What I could check in his words fitted in with what I knew to be true. Barbara New had written him a letter, because I had seen it arrive. Yet her voice, when she mentioned her client in the neighborhood, had carried a suggestion of long acquaintance, even intimacy. Now his whole manner disowned it.

"You're very fond of Folly House, aren't you?" I asked slowly.

"Love it," he said briefly. "I love the house, the woods, the soil itself."

"People matter more than places," I answered, wondering whether he had killed two people to preserve Folly House.

"Well, of course they do," he said, and this time I seemed to have surprised him. "But houses last longer."

It was as if he had given me a blow in the face. Yes, I thought, this man would sacrifice both Piers and Barbara New for Folly House if he had to do it.

And then I thought, If he killed her, then he knows she's dead. But he does not know that I know. So I tested him.

"I'd like to meet her," I said. "I'd like to talk to her myself. I've got some questions."

His expression didn't change. "Try her. But she seems unreliable. Doesn't keep her appointments."

I said, "She's dead. She kept *that* appointment."

"But that's terrible news. It distresses me very much. Are you sure?" He seemed full of shock and surprise.

"Oh yes, I'm very sure. I almost saw it happen. A road accident in Brayford. Just like Piers."

"Just like Piers?" he repeated.

155

We were standing very close, and seemingly spontaneously, he reached out and took my hand. If we had gone on talking, I think we might have come to some truth between us. The whole truth, perhaps. But we were interrupted by a sudden commotion, the first I had ever heard in that quiet house.

Someone was hammering on a door, a distant door, hammering and shouting. The dogs at once set up their own clamor and bolted in the direction of the noise.

With an exclamation, Kit went after them. "Stay here," he called to me.

I waited a second, then followed.

Ahead of me I saw Kit beginning to run as the banging and shouting mounted to a peak. We went through a dark passage and came out into what was clearly the kitchen.

It was huge, with whitewashed walls and stoneflagged floor, pleasantly cool now but I could imagine it would be freezing cold in winter. Old-fashioned as the room looked at a first glance, it was lined with sleek modern equipment. I remembered that Folly House had once been a restaurant.

The noise was coming from a door that led to the garden. The dogs were already lined up on our side of the door, leaping and barking.

"Shut up," shouted Kit; he had to shout to be heard above the noise. The dogs lay down in a half-circle, eyes bright, momentarily quiet.

I stood well back, watching.

Kit drew back the heavy bolts and pulled at the door. It creaked noisily and scraped the stone flags as it came back, suggesting disuse.

"Come on in, Joss," said Kit Temple in a stern if friendly tone. "You know we never use this door. What is it now?"

156

Old Joss was through the door in an instant, seizing hold of Kit's arm. "Oh, I'm glad you're awake and up, Mr. Temple, sir."

"Of course I am," said Kit with some irritation.

"It's coming on bad, sir. I can smell the fire and I hear it too. Crackle and snap. And my Mary's there with me, too." He cast a frightened glance behind him. "Can't you see it, sir, shining through the darkness?"

It was clear, gray daylight.

"No dark," said Kit patiently. "Come on in, Joss."

Joss pulled at his arm. "Come, please, sir. The fire's growing with every breath I draw. I can feel it in my lungs, scorching hot. I'm there in the middle. All round me there's fire." He kept looking behind him.

"You're in here, Joss."

Joss hardly seemed to hear. "I've Mary to think of. Can't you hear her crying?" Tears were pouring down his own cheeks now. "Ah sir, if you've any heart in you, come to the fire and get us out."

"You are out," said Kit soothingly. "We got you out. You remember now." He got his arm free and tried to use it to urge the man into the room. "Come in and sit down now."

He glanced round and saw me. "Give me a hand, will you?" Slowly I came over to where the pair of them stood. "He gets like this sometimes. Well, he drinks a bit, I think, and that starts him off."

Joss was standing still, a puzzled look on his face; he was shaking from head to foot.

"The fire's over now, old man," said Kit. "No more fire."

"No, you don't seem to understand, it's never out, not really out. Sometimes you think it is, and you think, Joss, it's safe, the fire's all gone now, but it's there waiting, ready to spring up. It's always there in hiding, always

157

ready to come alive again. A little heart of it is always there. You can hear it singing. I've often heard it. Have you heard it?"

"No," said Kit. "Not me, I've never heard it."

"But now it's getting ready to shout." He was shouting himself again, and crying. Tears were pouring down his face. "You should listen, I tell you. And Mary's calling with it. She can't help but call, she's burning too."

Kit gave an exclamation under his breath. To me he said, "You'll find some brandy and a glass on a table in the library. Bring some back here, will you? I don't know if it will make him better or worse, but we'll try it."

When I got back he had Joss in a chair at the kitchen table and was sitting beside him talking in a low voice. He was being very gentle and quiet. He took the glass from me without a word and took a sip himself, and offered a sip to Joss. Turn by turn, they drank it.

Soon they had sunk into a companionable silence, punctuated by grunts of conversation. I sat opposite them at the table and watched. I have never seen anyone so gently and quietly calmed as Joss was by Kit. You remember Kipling's phrase about Judy O'Grady and the Colonel's Lady? I saw it was true of men also. As they drank and offered each other odd phrases as the coin of conversation, they were brothers under the skin, this pair, old countryman and soldier of fortune.

Joss communicated with Kit in a way I could not do, although Kit's and my communication was, as I saw in a flash, through the skin.

I suppose it was in that moment I saw what Kit was to me. Or could have been. A man to love.

It was something for me to discover I could nourish such feeling for a man I thought a murderer. Already the figure of Piers was receding into the distance, becoming insubstantial, a ghost. Simon had killed him with a kiss.

But I didn't love Simon. I couldn't. The sensation that Piers lived again in Kit was too much for me.

"I'm coming round to myself again now, Mr. Kit," I heard Joss mutter. "It's going off, that bad feeling. The fire's out. I know that now. I let you down, Mr. Kit."

"You didn't let me down, Joss."

"Maybe I should leave off working in the woods. I'm no good to you there." Remorse and self-recrimination had set in.

"You're not to leave off, Joss. And you are a help. There's going to be more work for you now. We'll be getting things going again. I know I've let them run down but there will be some more money now."

I heard that: Money from the sale of the Chinese jar, I thought. Something had happened to him that was soon to free Kit Temple to sell the jar and use the money for Folly House. What that something was, I did not know, but I knew it must be connected somehow with the death of Barbara New. Or the life of Barbara New, I added to myself.

I heard Joss speaking in eager response to Kit. I must have made a movement, for Joss saw me then. "Is that your good lady?" he said.

"No. I'm not married. You know that, Joss," Kit reminded him gently.

He peered at me. "I know her face. I've seen her in the woods."

"I daresay you have."

"You should be married, sir. 'Tis better to be married than to . . .'" He stopped.

"Now don't start that again, Joss," said Kit, even more gently than before.

Joss got up. "I'll be going now. I believe I could do with a sleep."

He shuffled forward, taking a look at me as he did so.

"Anyway, I know who you are now. You're the girl that cries under the tree with a hole in it. I know that tree."

I swallowed. "That's right," I said. It was funny to see myself so clearly as someone else saw me: the girl that cries under the tree. Had I done it so often?

He frowned. "There was someone looking for you the other day. A lad."

Simon, I thought.

But Joss went on. "He was looking for you. Said he'd been waiting and looking and you'd never come. Ah, he has hungry eyes."

I could feel my heart stop and then give a great beat to compensate. I think the color must have ebbed from my cheeks, because Kit looked at me sharply.

"Are you all right?"

I nodded. The fact was I could hardly speak. "Who was he, this boy you saw?" I managed to say. "Did you know him?"

Joss paused for a moment, then a look of sad, piercing sanity came into his eyes. Unexpectedly he said, "The truth is I don't really know if he was there or not. Sometimes, like with my Mary, I can't tell."

Our silence was punctured by the urgent ringing of the doorbell.

"Damn. I'll have to go and answer." Kit disappeared, back through the kitchen toward the hall, the dogs following, all barking.

I waited for a moment, then followed him. I heard him open the front door and I heard the mutter of voices. A man's voice; then Kit answered again. I couldn't hear what he said. Then I heard him say clearly, "Yes, do come in."

Two men and Kit went into the library. I saw just their backs as the door closed behind them.

I went quietly past the library door and looked out the

160

hall window: an official-looking black car was parked outside. To me it had an unmistakable look. I was quite sure it was a police car, and that the men who had just arrived were policemen.

I tried to listen at the library door, but beyond the low mutter of voices I could hear nothing.

Thoughtfully I went back to the kitchen, where old Joss was still standing. He was beginning to show signs of confusion again.

"Is it the fire? The fire has begun again, the woods are burning," he said as soon as he saw me.

"No, no fire, nothing is burning," I reassured him gently. "You go on home now, Joss."

"But there is the comet. I think it might burn the woods. The animals think so." He shook his head.

"No, no," I assured him. "It's harmless. You need not fear it. All that will happen is that it will come closer and look bigger, and then it will go away."

I gave him a gentle push toward the door and closed it behind him, but did not bolt it. I might need a quick way out.

Kit Temple was shut up in the library with the police. I intended to make my search of the house.

Hanging on a hook beside her colored apron was the bunch of keys I had seen Mrs. Gamble carrying. I took them down, closed the kitchen door quietly behind me, and made my way through the house and up the stairs.

I was taking a gamble, running a risk, and I knew it, but I didn't care.

Seven

———◆———

How hard it is sometimes to do what you want to do, to do what you know must be done. I was full of resolve, but I found myself creeping with limbs like lead up the stairs.

I had been up here once before. Nothing seemed changed. The life that I sensed was beginning again downstairs had not reached this upper floor. All was quiet and untouched, with an air of having been deserted.

But so much had happened to me since that visit. Barbara New had come into my life and was now dead. The police were at this moment talking to Kit Temple. I was sure it was about the circumstances of her visit to Brayford. If that was so, the police must think her death was murder. She had been killed before she could talk to me about Piers and the sale at Mallards of the little bronze figure. I felt now that the ownership and sale of a Chinese jar made by a man called Wan Li who had lived four hundred years ago was also part of the mystery.

Ahead of me I could see nothing but the closed doors of the rooms on this floor, but I had a view up the stairwell to the next floor. The curtains and blinds were drawn so that a somber dusk lay over everything. In the distance I could see the pale gleam of an antique mirror.

I tried the doors. All now were unlocked, as if a slow opening-up process was beginning. All the rooms were furnished as bedrooms. When Folly House was made a country restaurant perhaps a small hotel had been intended also. The rooms were plain and neat, but only the one I had entered on my first visit had any character.

My eyes were getting used to the dim light by now, and standing in the threshold I could see the last room clearly. The dust sheets were off and the furniture stood unveiled. Not much there when all was said and done: a bed, a bureau with book-shelves above, and an easy chair, every piece of plain, good quality.

But without having to seek for a reason, I knew that this had been Piers's room. His use of it could only have been short, for Kit had not bought Folly House until after Piers and I had parted; and yet I felt his presence strongly.

I sat down on the bed and wondered why. The room had been stripped of all possessions, no physical traces of Piers remained, so why was I so sure? I could almost see him sitting in the armchair, laughing at me. In a strange way he was closer to me physically at that moment than I would have thought possible. He seemed to have come alive again, as if at any moment he might walk into the room again. It was an ordinary enough little room. I didn't suppose that Piers had ever spent more than a few days in it, and yet he was *here*.

But there was nothing to give me any clue about his

death, no piece of evidence of the sort I was looking for, that would shout at me and say, Yes, these are the signs of murder. I studied the room, convinced that there must be something there, and yet unable to find it.

I left the room, Piers's room it was to me now, and went up to the next floor. No curtains or blinds had been drawn on that floor, because there were none to draw; thus there was more light to see by, but there was less to see. The rooms here lay beneath the roof and perhaps had been meant for an earlier generation of servants to sleep in. One larger room, which looked as though it had been made by knocking two rooms into one, had been used as a nursery, judging by the bars on the window. All the rooms were swept and neat but quite empty, except for one room at the end of the corridor, which contained trunks and valises. There was also a pile of packing cases, which were now empty but looked as though they had contained books. I knew already that the Temple family had lived abroad a lot—they had been an Army family— and you could see this way of life reflected in their battered luggage, some of which looked as though it had belonged to several generations, good solid leather stuff handed down from father to son.

I shut this door behind me and walked toward the stairs. The whole floor felt "neutral," if I can express it that way, as if it had absolutely no information to offer me one way or the other.

That shows how one can jump to conclusions: I shan't do so again.

Halfway down the stairs from the top floor I heard sounds of departure from below. Voices, the dogs barking, the bang of the door, followed by the sound of the car's engine. The police were gone.

Kit must have been looking for me. I heard him calling: "Christabel? Christabel, are you still here?"

I drew back up the stairs, still and quiet.

"Christabel?" He was calling up the stairs now, but he made no move up them. One of the dogs came running up the stairs. I could hear the thud of his paws, accompanied by excited barks. In another moment he would have found me.

"Come down, you idiot," I heard Kit call out. "She's not up there. She's gone off, I suppose." He didn't sound pleased.

I came down the rest of the flight and stood in the upper hall. On the wall at the end I could just make out my own figure in the oval mirror.

The door of Piers's room seemed to have swung open, so I went to close it. Out of the corner of my eye I was watching my image in the mirror. In the antique glass my reflection seemed to waver and change shape.

It was then I became certain that someone was up there with me.

In that first moment of knowing, it was hard to tell which sense had alerted me—whether I had heard some soft secret noise, or had seen a flash of movement. I stood there, absolutely still, waiting.

"Who's there?" I said softly.

A brief silence answered.

"Piers?" I called. "Are you there?"

Why did I call his name? I shall never know, I did it so spontaneously and innocently. But innocence has never been any vindication. No, nor protection either.

Those who summon up ghosts deserve all they get, and I know now that when I cried out Piers's name, I called up anger.

"Piers," I said again, and then I stopped myself. Someone was there. I was quite sure of it.

In the mirror I had seen something or some person

165

move. Before my eyes part of the reflected image had melted away.

Stiffly, slowly, I walked to the end of the corridor and looked up the stairs.

Nothing. Nothing on the upper flight and nothing on the lower flight leading to the hall.

I continued on down to the hall with its lovely old rugs and antique oak chest, dark as ebony. I had a notion of movement, as if a shadow had crossed the floor. And had the library door been quietly closed?

I walked past, not even trying to listen. Either Kit was there, innocently sitting with his dogs, or he was listening for me.

So I went through to the kitchen again. I had noticed a door and wanted to see where it led.

I only half admitted it to myself, but of course I was looking for Piers. Rationality made me say that I was looking for clues to his murder. Really, I was looking for him. I was looking for him in the obstinate, dogged, unreasoning way one looks for a lost object even though one knows in one's heart it is gone beyond recall.

This disbelief of death might be part of grieving, I told myself, an essential step in mourning; but it might also be a healthy incredulity.

In the kitchen again I had the feeling that someone was with me. Or close behind. I went back to the kitchen door and looked down the corridor that led back to the living part of the house. The door which separated the two regions and which I had left open was closed, that was the only difference.

It could have swung to of its own volition. I told myself it would have been more alarming if I had left it closed and found it open.

I went back to the kitchen and took a second look round. On the table were the glasses used by Kit and

166

Joss. I took them up and dumped them in the sink. Around the sink was a sort of enclave, not of civilization, one could hardly call it that, but of feminine occupation, laid out, no doubt, by Mrs. Gamble. A dish cloth, a sponge mop, a metal pan cleaner and a bottle of cleanser called Clenso, together with a rolled up apron, bore her signs. I could see there was a huge and beautiful dishwasher, but she chose not to use it. Likewise, deposited near her apron was a cushion kneeler for polishing the floor (which was rather unpolished) whereas I was sure that locked away in that closet by the back door was the most modern of electric polishers. Mrs. Gamble had a style of her own, as I had gathered early on from the sight of the coffee tray she presented to Kit and me, and impersonal efficiency was not it. The exact opposite might be a better way of putting it.

I didn't think I would find anything in the kitchen; Mrs. Gamble, with her personalized inefficiency, would have exorcized it. I saw why Joss had dared to come and have his mad fit today: it wasn't a day Mrs. Gamble came. He was taking advantage of her absence to indulge *his* ghost, just as I was to indulge mine. And Kit, what was Kit doing? Playing host to both our ghosts?

But I did, as it happens, look over the kitchen, and there I found a pile of old newspapers, all going back to the summer of last year. I flipped through them. As far as I could see life had stopped for Kit Temple over a year ago.

I opened a door in the kitchen: it led to a narrow passage from which opened several antique pantries, once designed to be the workplaces of housemaids and pantry boys. Now they were empty and dusty.

The passage was closed by yet another door.

I tried the handle: it was locked. I studied it. The door was old, as old as the house, I thought, and the lock was old. At a later date, in fact fairly recently as I judged, someone had added two bolts, on this the kitchen side of the door, as if to make sure that whoever or whatever was inside the room stayed there. These bolts were now drawn back.

I looked around for a key, but although there was a hook beside the door which looked as though a key might have hung there, none hung on it now.

The lock looked very old and frail, as if rust and habit held it together more than solid metal. I went back into the kitchen, found a sturdy knife in a drawer, and came back. Then I stuck the blade between door and lock and exerted leverage. I heard a snap; I looked to see whether knife or lock had gone first, thinking the chances about even. It was the lock. I withdrew the knife and pushed at the door, which swung open before me.

A breath of dank, dusty air floated out to meet me, chill even in that heat. On the threshold I shivered. But I went in, closing the door quietly behind me. I was in what had once been, in the days of great Edwardian shooting parties, the gun room, and indeed one or two sporting rifles still rested in the racks and Kit Temple occasionally used them.

Slowly I looked around me.

There was one small window in the room, and that was high up on one wall, covered by a grating. By the light that came through it I saw bare walls and a stoneflagged floor. Both looked gray, but perhaps it was just the light. The floor was empty.

Against one wall was a barred structure reaching right to the ceiling, like a giant baby's playpen.

It looks like a cage, I thought.

Then I looked round the room and thought about those bolts on the outer door. "It's a prison," I said aloud.

There was a strange sour smell on the air, more animal than human: it was the smell of imprisonment.

I went back to the thing on the wall. "And that's a cage: a man-cage."

Perhaps I said it half in joke, but the impression of a cell was heightened by what was inside: a flat, palletlike mattress of thick dark rubber on the floor.

Investigation showed me that there was a kind of sliding door, like a hatch, on one side of the cage. You had to slide it upward and crawl in. Like an animal, I thought.

I lifted it and scrambled through. I had a purpose; there was a wooden box near the rubber pallet, and even from outside I could see that into it had been thrown roughly, carelessly, a jumbled assortment of someone's personal possessions.

My heart banging in my throat, I saw a pair of rubber sneakers, once white, now dirty and old. A torn sweater made of good quality gray wool. When I could bring myself to touch it, I could feel it was cashmere. A raincoat, a Burberry, again of good quality although dirty, had been rolled up and thrust into the box. Underneath the clothing I could see books, notebooks, folders of papers, together with a small transistor radio and a football. Everything looked abandoned, put away forever.

Was he dead then, the owner of these possessions? Ask a silly question, get a silly answer. I picked up the sweater; it had an embroidered name tape sewn into the neckband: Piers Temple.

But, of course, I had known these were Piers's possessions. That was why I had entered the cage.

When had his property been placed here? I asked myself. Before or after his death? Was it possible he had been imprisoned here? How *could* that be, and why? I asked myself desperately, one terrible question arising in my mind as another subsided.

169

I dragged the box more into the light, but it was still difficult to see well in the semi-dark, so I pulled the box out through the hatch and into the middle of the room.

Then I thrust my hand in and drew out a leatherbound book, a diary. I started to turn the leaves, my hands trembling and my eyes blurring with tears. The papers were covered in Piers's large, neat hand.

I knew that at last I had a chance to read the record of Piers's last days as he had recorded them. I crouched there, reading.

At a first quick glance it looked as if the diary was simply a record of his work, of lectures attended and books read. I couldn't see my name at all. Indeed, no one's name appeared. It was as if Piers had been intent to record only the outer surface of his life, and to conceal the inner. Yet what right had I to believe I knew the secret Piers? Perhaps all I saw here was the real Piers and there was no richer inner person. If so, the years had truly parted us.

But the very last entry was different. It was undated, since it seemed to sprawl across several days, with Piers's handwriting getting larger and larger all the time. The writing, this large, urgent writing, began in the space devoted to Wednesday, August 11, and carried on through Thursday and Friday till it finished up on Saturday. After Saturday there was nothing. Sunday was blank and all successive days after that. Forever.

I read:

I have started to think about seeing Christabel again. The time is coming closer, not so long, although I suppose the last few weeks will seem long enough. Funny, I rely upon her coming. I know she will. I wonder if she knows the same about me? I trust to her loyalty. I thought about her a lot lately, perhaps I've never stopped. Of course, there have been other girls I've looked at and found attractive, made love to a bit, but at the back of it all there's only ever been Christabel. I suppose I'm just a natural romantic. I wonder if she's been the same? I do trust to her. I find myself using that word a lot. Probably because I have begun to wonder if I *can* trust someone else. I begin to have very definite suspicions there. I suppose I'll have to do something. I wish Kit wasn't in such an awkward mood.

Tears gathered in my eyes; I knew now that Piers had loved me as I had loved him, to know it was to feel both pain and happiness, because he was gone. Halfway down the page there was one sentence in big letters:

The need to see Christabel is now paramount.

So totally engrossed was I, every sense absorbed in my reading, that I heard nothing.

Suddenly I became conscious that I was not alone. Someone was standing behind me.

I tried to stand up but a hand pushed me back.

I had an instant flood of recognition. I know who this is, I thought. Then pain shattered my head into darkness.

There was a scream echoing round and round in the black void.

Eight

❖

The screaming had stopped and I was far away, in a quiet country, where no sun shone and only starlight illuminated the land. In this I rested for a while. Then the starlight died away to be replaced by a gray dawn. "Star light, far light. Day light, dead light," I heard myself saying aloud. It sounded a good sentence, and for a moment I was pleased with it. I stayed with it for a little while, enjoying my wit, then I opened my eyes.

Or perhaps they had been open all the time and sight had just returned to them. Now I saw a gray ceiling; I was lying on my back, staring up. It took a bit of time for me to recognize it for what it was. Out of context (and I had been snatched out of context) a ceiling is an anonymous sheet.

Suddenly I was back in a full state of consciousness, sharply aware of an aching head, and knew that the last thing I had heard had been my own screaming voice.

I put up my hand and touched my head: I had been hurt. I remember saying the words plaintively, like a child. I had a momentary hallucination at this point that I was a head without a body. "So that's what Humpty Dumpty is all about," I said aloud. But just saying the words aloud was enough to put the fantasy to flight: I was stone-cold awake.

I pushed myself into a sitting position. A coherent picture was taking shape in my mind. My exploration had brought me down here to this strange room. I had found a box of Piers's possessions, and while I was looking at his diary someone had come up behind me and knocked me out.

"And it was no ghost, either." Gently, I touched my head: there was a lump, though no blood. I had no idea how long I had been unconscious, but looking at the quality of the light in the room, which as far as I could judge had hardly changed, it had not been for long.

I stood up, staggering momentarily, then steadying myself against the box, and walked across the room to the door.

The door was stuck fast. I shook the handle and pushed, but although it seemed to yield a little, at top and bottom it held firm. I remembered those outer bolts and knew that I was bolted inside.

I had walked into a prison.

Hammering on the door and shouting was probably going to be no good, but I did it anyway. I called and banged on the door panels till my voice was rough and my hands sore. My head had ached already and it was not improved. Now I felt sick as well.

All in all I was in poor shape by the time I stopped. Kit either hadn't heard me or didn't want to hear.

I sat down on the floor and leaned my back against the wall. My eyes fell on the box of Piers's property. An urgent question dragged me to my feet again, and I staggered over to the box.

The diary, Piers's diary, had gone.

I made a hasty search, but it wasn't in the box, nor had I expected it to be there. Whoever had hit me on the head and locked me into the room had taken it. To me the inescapable conclusion was that it had contained evidence about Piers's death.

I was lucky not to be dead. But there was more than one way of dying.

I hammered on the door. "Let me out, let me out," I shouted. "I'm not going to stay in here and starve to death." I was sobbing with anger. Yes, and with fear too. I felt as though the door of a trap had slid down behind me, and I was inside like an animal. What does the rat feel when it is inside the trap and begins to die? I felt I knew.

"Let me out. Out, out. I'm not one of your animals that's going to die quietly. I'll shout and shout."

Sweat was pouring off me. My throat was parched. Suddenly I was exhausted. I staggered back toward the cage, slid the door open, and with a last burst of energy dragged the box into the aperture to wedge the door. Then I dropped onto the pallet. There are times when mind and body demand oblivion, but before sleep claimed me, I caught a strong, pungent scent from the pallet, as if the last occupant . . . I never completed the thought; I was asleep.

When I awoke, the room was dark. I had a sense of having been asleep for some time. Long enough, anyway, for day to have faded into evening.

I felt alert and in command of myself. For a moment I did not move but lay quietly on my back staring upward. I could see the square of the window and glimpse the moon riding behind a cloud. A fan of cool air fell on my face. So there could be no glass in the window; it was simply an open square, high in the wall.

I thought about that for a moment. Then I put the thought aside, because I wanted to think about something else.

I didn't know who had followed me, who had hit me, but Kit Temple had to be regarded as a suspect. There was no one else in the house, was there?

It was his house. Wasn't he therefore the most likely person to have followed me about?

Nor did I know why I had been attacked, not precisely, but Piers's diary had had something to do with it. I bitterly regretted the loss of the diary.

I stood up and looked at the window in the wall. It was high up and, although I knew now I could certainly climb out through it, I would have needed wings to get up there.

Wait a minute, though. The bars of the cage ran right up to the ceiling, and from the top of the one nearest the wall it would be possible, just possible, to reach across to the hole in the wall.

I tested the bar and found it solid enough. The question was, could I shin up it, hand over hand, pushing up with my feet?

Up the greasy pole, I thought, but it was worth a try.

I took my shoes off and tied them round my neck. I thought that bare feet would be best. My hands were sweating; I rubbed them dry on my skirt and reached. Up. I took a good grip and jumped my feet onto the pole. Slowly I edged myself upward, inch by inch. Soon my shoulders and arms were aching desperately. I slipped once, nearly to the floor, but I hauled myself back again.

At the top I hung on painfully and looked across to the window. My heart sank. The distance was greater than I had thought, and even if I did jump across there was nothing to catch onto. But the brick was rough and irregular; I might be able to get a grip.

I leaned across and managed to fasten on with my left hand to the rudimentary windowsill. Then in one swift continuous movement, so that the momentum would carry me forward, I pushed with my feet against the bar and swung my right arm and hand to a position parallel with my left arm. Even as I did that I drew myself up.

I was crouching, precariously, swaying back and forth on the sill of the window. My head and shoulders and knees all bunched together. Even now I don't know how I did it, my body seemed to act spontaneously and with a rhythm of its own. Perhaps in moments of crisis it always does.

I looked to the ground outside. At once I felt more cheerful. Because the ground rose toward the woods, this window was nearer the ground outside than to the floor inside. And the jump was on to soft earth. It looked like a potato bed. I was looking down on the kitchen garden.

In the sky the moon and the comet rode majestically together. I had just a moment to look before I leapt. As I leapt spontaneously I thought: if I could get out this way, then why didn't Piers if he was imprisoned there?

I fell awkwardly, landing in a sprawling heap with one leg twisted underneath me. It hurt. Slowly I raised myself, testing my leg and wincing a little.

"Damn, oh damn."

I was sitting there rubbing my leg when I heard the dogs barking. Suddenly they were all round me, leaping at me and barking.

Where they went, Kit Temple was not far behind.

"Quiet, dogs," he said, suddenly appearing round the corner of the house.

"What happened to that story they only barked when

you left?" I said, flexing my leg, attack being the best method of attack.

"And what are you doing?"

"Getting out of your house," I said.

"Then you are leaving," he observed, with deceptive mildness.

"If I can."

He didn't answer directly; he was watching me. "Is your ankle broken?"

"No, only sprained. I can manage." I took a hobbled step or two.

"I think not," he said gravely, holding out an arm. "Here, let me help you."

"No, thank you." I tried very hard to stay upright and push away from him, but he ignored my efforts and put an arm round me.

"You're trembling."

"With anger," I said from between clenched teeth.

He steadied me. "What *were* you doing?"

"I told you: escaping."

"But you went home hours ago. Did you come back?"

I didn't answer but tried to start walking home to the observatory. This was a mistake.

"Come on, I'll carry you back into the house." He bundled me up. One of the dogs growled in jealousy.

I still struggled. "No, please don't. I tell you I can walk." I was beginning to get a sense of what hour it was; I assessed it was just around midnight.

"Manifestly you can't." He was striding forward.

"I'll manage. You'd better put me down. I'm heavier than I look."

"You are, too," he added, after a pause. He took a few more steps. "I think I'll make it, though."

I didn't give up. "I want to go back through the woods. Back to the observatory."

"You'd much better stay the night in Folly House. I'll drive you back in the morning. Rest that foot. And when you're safely tucked up we can have a little chat about *what* you were doing," he added pleasantly.

Now that I was with Kit, in fact pressed closely against him, close enough (if reluctantly so) to feel the beat of his heart, I could not maintain the fantasies I had built up against him in that horrible room. I wanted so much to believe that the real Kit Temple was this solid, gentle, rational person I was with now. Let the monster I had invented be not real, I was really saying inside myself.

Yet at the same time I could not bring myself to trust him. Too many disquieting things had happened in his ambience.

He paused for a moment, to get his breath, I suppose, and still holding me firmly. "I am quite curious," he observed.

"I was jumping out of a sort of prison in your house, where I had been shut up. I was hit on the head."

"I know the room you mean, although not what you mean by prison," he said coolly. "What I don't know is what on earth you were doing down there."

"Looking, that's what I was doing. I was looking. I was looking at Piers's diary. I was going to find out why he was killed and who killed him when I was hit and the diary was taken from me."

It came out like an accusation, and he was not stupid, he got the implication. I was looking at him, my head twisted to see, and anger flashed at once into his face.

"Right." He lowered his arms; I won't say he dropped me, but I was deposited with some force. Dumped, say. "You want to walk home, well, you can do it."

I leaned against the wall and we stared at each other, as angry as we had ever been with each other.

"For some time now, slowly at first, I must admit, it

178

has been dawning on me that you think I killed my nephew. Oh yes, don't worry. You've made it beautifully plain. Even—" and he gave me a brilliant smile "—to someone who doesn't want to hear." The smile disappeared. "Because, you see, I had inside me the beginnings of a hope about you. I thought you were perfectly what I had always hoped to find."

I stared at him silently.

"Ridiculous, isn't it? Because I also thought you liked me too."

I was still silent. Then I turned and limped away through the garden and toward the woods.

My ankle was sore, but I could move. I turned at one point and looked back. He was standing there looking at me. Gritting my teeth, I plodded on.

I was already struggling up the path toward the woods when I heard the car's engine behind me. He had brought the Range-Rover over the uneven ground to reach me. He stopped the car just by me and held the door open.

"Get in. I'll drive you round by the road to the observatory."

"You must be mad to think I'd get in with you." I tried to trudge on.

"I know you're running away from me, but you might as well do it in comfort." He sounded amused.

"I'm managing, thank you."

"Rubbish." He jumped down and stood beside me. "You needn't be frightened."

"I'm not frightened."

"No? You needn't be. I'm not going to hurt you. Don't be stupid. Get in." He came toward me. "Come on, I'll help you in."

I braced myself against a tree, prepared to resist.

He looked nonplussed. "Christabel, I'm not sure what

you're thinking; I don't know what mad ideas you've got, but I want to help. You're in pain, I can see you are."

"I'll get back. In my own way."

"I don't think you will." He put a hand on me and I stiffened. He felt my reaction and drew back at once. "Well, all right, you don't like me to touch you." A line of white had appeared round his mouth. "Don't worry, I won't."

"No, no," I said, confused and embarrassed beyond anything I could have expected. "I don't want you to think . . ."

"Don't you?"

With a shrug, he turned back toward the Range-Rover. Something about his arrogant self-possession, when my own was shattered, got under my skin. "What was it you did to Piers?" I shouted. "What did you do?"

He spun round. "I'll tell you the truth: I did nothing to Piers. Yes, we had a disagreement, hardly even a quarrel, but I thought I had something to blame myself for. Now I don't think so. Satisfied?"

"I don't know," I said reluctantly.

"Well, it's all I'm telling you. Now will you get in the car, or shall I have to lift you in?"

Silently I hobbled over toward the Range-Rover. My ankle was now very sore, but he let me make it on my own, only putting out a hand to steady me as I climbed in. His hand on my bare skin felt warm and dry. I turned to look at him, and he drew away at once. "Silly creature," he said, gently and with amusement, much as he might have said it to one of his dogs. And I swear he said it fondly. Tears pricked behind my eyes. He turned and saw.

"I only ever cry from anger," I said fiercely.

Miserably I sat beside him as he backed the car between two trees and swung the wheel. The car made nothing of the rough terrain, it was like a little tank. We bumped down to where the drive was, circled the house, and then out onto the road.

We didn't speak. When we got to the old observatory he drove smartly up to the steps and stopped. Still without a word.

I got out. "Thanks," I said, and turned and stumbled to the door.

"I'll come over later and see how you are," he called after me.

"Don't bother, I'm fine."

"I'll come anyway." I heard the car move away fast.

Simon came calling for me almost as soon as I got in; I knew he would. I was standing in the kitchen drinking a long draft of cold water.

"Where have you been? I've been watching and waiting."

"In Folly House." I was pleased by my careful use of the preposition: it was certainly "in" rather than "at."

"What happened? Something happened, look at you." He was studying me. "Your face—there's a bruise on your temple—and you're limping. It's your leg: you're lame. You *have* been in trouble."

"Yes. You could call it that." I drained the glass.

"I told you not to go there. What happened?"

"I was hit on the head while I was reading a diary of Piers's. Then I was locked in a downstairs room like a prison."

"And your leg?"

"Oh, I did that getting out." I tried to sound light. Simon was not amused. He poured out questions.

"Who attacked you? Did you see?" And when I was silent: "It *must* have been *him*."

"I honestly don't know. I don't know what happened exactly. Or why. I can't make sense of it. Perhaps it was

181

Kit Temple. Do you know that legend of the god Janus, who had two faces, one smiling and one threatening? He's like that to me. Sometimes he seems so *good*, and then . . ." I turned away.

"You mean you don't understand him," said Simon scornfully.

"Not him nor Folly House. I don't know what he meant to do with me. Perhaps leave me to die." In spite of the continuing heat, I shivered. "But my body would have been found. It must have been."

"He may have meant to burn the place down." Simon looked out the window to the woods, still silvered by the moon. "It's very hot, haven't you noticed? A fire would be very plausible. That comet makes one seem almost inevitable. And then your leg . . . you might have killed yourself with a drop like that."

"I didn't, though. Good night, Simon. Go away now." I gave him a little push. "I'm going to have a long, long shower and wash my hair and go to bed and sleep. I'm glad you're here. It makes me feel *safe*."

A wind was beginning to blow again even though it was so hot. All that night it howled and moaned through the trees.

It was only in the morning I discovered I had lost the keys to Folly House. Lost or stolen, they were no longer in my possession. I couldn't get back in there now, I was shut out. At the time, it seemed symbolic: later, I saw the real, the practical, significance of my loss.

The heat remained intense, but in the morning the wind had died down again, although occasionally the tops of the tallest trees tossed angrily as if a sudden gust had caught them. The birds were quiet, and every so often an animal would come to the edge of Axwater, drink, and melt back into the woods again. The comet was very visible now, night and day.

I took some books down to the lake and sat there in the shade, pretending to work. I had my eyes closed a good deal of the time, but I wasn't sleeping. I wasn't tired. An inner excitement burned inside me, giving me energy. I was thinking: I was debating whether to go to the police with my suspicions. But they were just that—suspicions.

Across the lake I could see Simon's encampment. He was working there today, or like me, was pretending to. He seemed to be spending a lot of the time staring into the lake. At intervals he waved to me, and I waved a languid hand back.

Presently he came across and sat at my feet, looking at me. I knew he wanted to talk about last night, and I knew I didn't want to.

"How's your leg?"

"Not bad." I flexed the ankle, which was swollen but usable.

"You're buttoning it all up, not talking. That's bad, you ought to talk. Anyway, to me."

"Why you?" I was pretending to read because I wanted him to go away.

"Because I can help. I have helped already. I told you to watch Kit Temple and you did."

"Yes, I did," I agreed.

"He must have come in, seen you reading Piers's diary, and knocked you out before you could read what Piers had to say. It would have accused him, that's why."

"If the diary was so dangerous, I don't know why he hadn't destroyed it, then," I said slowly. "He had it there in his possession all the time."

"It wasn't dangerous to him till you started to read it," said Simon.

"Mm—perhaps you're right. I ought to have asked him straight out. But he got angry and I became angry myself. Perhaps I will ask him, perhaps I'll go back and have it all out."

Part of me wanted desperately to do this, and part of me didn't.

"For heaven's sake don't," said Simon hastily.

I was silent, not looking at him. I wanted to say to Simon, But I have a weapon, a very strong weapon, the man's in love with me.

"I think I know a bit of the background, something of what lies behind it all," I said. "It concerns the sale of precious objects to Mallards, the auction people in London. Do you remember the 'object of value' that Piers left me? It was a bronze statuette, and this was sold, too. Barbara New was coming to tell me about it. She never did. She was stopped. A Chinese jar was sold also, or that is my guess. I believe there must have been other objects too."

I stopped, I had never before been quite so explicit to Simon, never said quite so much, but his quietness had led me on. I could see he thought it all important.

"*She* thought I had sold the bronze and got the money for it," I suddenly said. "I wish I knew *why* she thought that. Because I didn't and couldn't have."

My energy burst out and I got up and started to pace up and down. "Yes, that's important," I said. "Don't you see? It's a totally *different* sort of fact from knowing the bronze and the jar were sold (which I believe) because I can *prove* it's a lie: I was in the States when the sale was on. Far, far away, and unknowing. I didn't even know Piers was dead. I can *prove* it."

And then, because I was so excited, I let out what I did not mean to let out. "Kit Temple's in love with me," I said. "Did you know that? I'm sorry. I shouldn't have said that. It's probably not true." But I knew it was,

184

whatever it meant, whatever his love was, I had it. It was mine.

Simon had gone very white. "I could kill him. If he lays a finger on you, I will kill him."

"You look more as if you'd like to kill *me*," I observed.

He glared at me: "Don't mock me."

Our eyes met, I stared gravely back, and eventually he gave a smile. "Good," I said. "One enemy is enough. I felt more frightened of you then than of Kit Temple."

"So you should," he said, standing. "I'm off for a bit. Brayford, then London. Business about my Himalayan trip. Look after yourself."

"You're really going then?" I stood up too. "I mean to India?"

"Think so. Looks like it. Oh, by the way, there was a woman kept telephoning while you were away yesterday. Wonder she hasn't tried again today."

"Who was it?"

"Didn't say. But she sounded as though she was crying."

"Crying?" I remembered another telephone call then and what I had heard. Could it be Catherine? "It might be my sister."

"She cries, does she?"

"It's said she's doing so at the moment." I frowned.

"Perhaps it was her. Come to think of it, her voice did sound like yours." He sounded uninterested in Catherine, as if no tears would touch *him*. "Come with me, Christabel. Why don't you? Let's go away now and never come back."

I didn't answer; probably he didn't expect me to. He gave me a kiss, a long, full, loving kiss such as I might once have enjoyed.

"Miss Glacier's back, I see," he said, drawing away.

I didn't answer, although he waited as if he hoped I

185

would speak. Finally he said, "Look—here's a telephone number for you to call if you want me." He sounded impatient. "It's the post office in Steeple Minden. I'll be in and out of there for a bit, settling things. You can get me if you want to change your mind." He thrust a piece of paper at me.

I took it silently, and he strode off without another word; I watched him go.

Across the water Simon's little encampment looked lonely in the sunshine, and also sad, as if a brave attempt had foundered. Simon had spoken cheerful words about his project, but I wondered. After a while I walked round the lake and went to look.

Apart from his tents there was very little to see. All his personal possessions had gone; I supposed he had moved them into the observatory. And would I continue to house them if he went to India? And for how long? I should have to ask him about that. I was beginning to realize that there were a lot of unspoken questions in my relationship with Simon, and most of them my fault. Still, this place did look as if he'd moved out, looked more deserted somehow than I would have expected.

There was a bit of old newspaper flying about the camp. It was filled with headlines about the comet. People were talking about it now as it got close. I picked up the piece of newspaper and thrust it into my pocket to tidy it away. It was the only piece of litter in Simon's camp, and perhaps a symbolic one.

My head ached, and my ankle was sore, but in spite of the events of yesterday I had no sense of personal danger. I did have a sensation as if someone was watching, but I dismissed it as fancy, a hangover from yesterday. Here I could stand on the sloping turf above Axwater and look around me and see that no one was there.

Then a little dog came running out of the woods from

the direction of Folly House. I recognized one of Kit Temple's dogs. Soon it was joined by another, and then another. Their appearance was an announcement I could read accurately enough. Presently, without surprise, I saw Kit Temple's tall figure appear on the path behind them.

The little dogs, who usually took almost no notice of me, now rushed up and began circling around me and giving tiny leaps in the air, barking all the time with excitement.

"Down, you brutes," shouted their master. Immediately they crouched in quiet little heaps on the ground, ears cocked, eyes concentrated on him. I waited in my little protective circle—I supposed I was being protected. Or guarded? Either way, it wouldn't have been easy for me to get away.

"I told you I'd come to see how you were," he said as soon as he drew close enough.

"My ankle's better."

"And you? Yes, you look better. I had to come to talk to you. I couldn't talk yesterday when you were so emotional and angry. I didn't mean to frighten you in any way. I don't know how I have. God, it's not what I want." His voice was serious. "Can't you trust me, Christabel? I'm not a criminal."

"Everyone asks me to trust them," I said. "But there's a terrible lot of violence around."

"If you'd just keep still for a while and listen to your instincts, I think they would tell you whom to trust."

"Meaning you?"

"I hope so."

I was very conscious of him looking at me; I was the first to turn away. "Oh, I wouldn't trust to my instincts," I said. "They're not reliable."

"Aren't they? I think they are." He dropped down on

187

to the turf. "Come on, sit down and have a cigarette and be reasonable."

"I don't smoke much." But I sat down.

"Neither do I. But there *are* times . . ."

We smoked for a while in silence, a peaceful, companionable silence. "That's better," he said. "You're coming round. Now listen to me, Christabel: I'm as concerned as you are about Piers's death and how it happened. I admit I didn't let myself think of it clearly before, but now you've dragged everything out into the open, it's got to be faced. And I mean to get to the bottom of what's happened. Apart from anything else, until Piers's ghost is laid there can't be anything real between you and me."

"And could there be?"

"Oh yes, I'm sure of it. You're sure of it, too. That's what I meant about instincts."

He sounded very certain of himself and of me too. I tried to repress what I felt to be an onward rush of emotion carrying me forward faster than I wanted. "I'd rather rely on reason."

"Yes, you're a very rational creature, Christabel, but I think that if you look at what's been happening, it's when you've clung to reason you've gone wrong, and when you've followed your instinct you've been right." He scrambled to his feet. "No, I'm not going to say any more. Just think about whom you've really trusted and don't blind yourself with reason." I got up too, and faced him. I wasn't as tall, but I was standing higher up the slope, so our eyes were level. We were very close. I thought he was going to move away without saying another word, but he turned back.

"Christabel, I don't think you realize the effect you have had coming into this valley, stirring up things that have lain dormant, releasing energies, attracting emotions to yourself. You seem as vital and explosive a natural force as that comet above."

"I'm not usually like that," I said hesitantly. "It's as if so many things that were latent inside me have come to life since I came to Axwater—I can't account for it except to say that, somehow, it must be due to Piers."

Instead of laughing at me, he said, "Thank you for saying that, Christabel. I think it's the truest and wisest thing you've said. I believe it gives Piers back to us, and us to each other. I hope you'll come to see that. And that's what I meant about instinct."

"I still don't know the truth about Piers's death," I whispered. "And I must. I must."

"And you shall. But don't be afraid. Are you afraid?"

"I'm not sure. A bit uneasy, perhaps." I looked round me. Everything seemed tranquil.

"I could leave you the dogs."

I laughed, and shook my head. "I should have to look after them. And you know they wouldn't stay without you."

"I'll go then, Christabel. Together we'll clear up this whole business. I'm glad I came. You are glad, too, aren't you?"

I nodded. "Yes, I am." And suddenly it was true.

"Sure you don't want me to stay?"

"No." But as he left, and as I watched his tall figure and the flashing, darting forms of the little dogs disappear, I felt very lonely.

Also, and more curiously, I felt very alert, as if I ought to be watching for something, only I did not know what.

To exorcise this feeling I went back to the observatory. In any case, the heat was beginning to be too intense for comfort outside on the hill. Nevertheless, the sensation of surveillance persisted, and as I walked back I kept glancing over my shoulder.

As I got to the observatory step, a woman appeared in the open doorway and stood silently looking at me from behind great dark sunglasses. But of course I knew the cut of the dark-blue silk dress.

"Catherine!" I ran toward her.

I hugged her and kissed her. "I'm so glad to see you. How did you get here?"

"Drove. I've got the car parked down on the road. I walked up along the path."

"Why didn't you say you were coming?"

She was silent.

"Here, let me look at you. Come out from behind those glasses."

"No, I'm hiding."

"From me?" I was laughing at her.

"From you most of all."

I took a step back and looked at her again. "I believe you mean that."

"We'll talk about it." She turned and led the way back into the house.

There was a smell of fresh coffee. While she was waiting for me she had brewed some. Groceries were strewn on the table: a pot of Greek honey from Mount Hymettus, a small loaf of the special rye bread with caraway seeds baked in a little shop in Soho, a box of green figs—my sister Catherine's idea of a little breakfast.

"I shopped on the way," she said absently, pouring herself another cup of coffee. "Help yourself."

She hadn't left much in the pot, obviously she'd been at it some time, but I took what there was. The flavor, naturally, was excellent, nothing second-rate about Catherine.

Catherine took off her spectacles and laid them on the table. Her face looked thinner than I remembered, but she had made it up with her usual precision, the coloring of cheeks and eyes laid on as expertly as usual, and there was certainly no sign of the puffiness of tears around her eyes.

"Well, you don't look as if you'd been crying," I said.

"Look as if I'd been crying?" She repeated the words, as if she was savoring them. "Who said I had been?"

"A man called Ned."

"Ned? Oh, him. I've not been crying. And if I wanted to, I wouldn't cry in front of Ned. He's gone now, in case you wanted to know."

"I didn't really," I said carefully; I was treading warily with her.

"And I'm not going to cry in front of you. Wouldn't dream of it. No. I might go on my knees and grovel. Or I might bang my head on the floor and kowtow. That's what it's called, I believe. I don't suppose they do it now in China." She was talking in a hard, brittle voice.

"Catherine, what is all this?"

"You don't know? You haven't guessed?"

I shook my head.

"You would have done in time. So even in telling you now, I'm not doing anything very splendid." She was lashing herself with her own scorn. I couldn't bear to watch her; it was as if she were flaying herself.

"Catherine, please."

"It's about the sale of the little bronze statuette at Mallards. *Your* statue, but I sold it. Oh yes, me. The box was addressed to Miss C. Warwick. Could have been me, couldn't it? So I gave myself the benefit of the doubt, although I knew perfectly well it was your property. But I needed the money. Oh, I desperately needed the money. My business was nearly bankrupt. But a few thousand would see me through."

"Oh, Catherine, dearest," I implored. "Don't go on."

"I knew the bronze's value, you see. It's the sort of thing I *do* know."

"I'd have *given* it to you," I said.

"No, but would you have? I don't think so. Because it was from Piers, wasn't it? Oh, I knew all about that thing between you. You thought you had it all covered up and that no one knew. But you were like a baby trying to hide the fact it had won the fairy from the top of the Christmas tree. I knew, my darling. I just had to hope Piers was good enough for you. I suppose he was, but we shall never know now, shall we?"

Catherine was crying, whether for herself or for me, I could not tell. I sat there watching, dry-eyed.

"Oh, I knew what I was doing," she went on, "but it wasn't till I fell in love myself that I realized quite what I'd done. I didn't mind being criminous, you see, but I couldn't bear to be cruel. I found it all quite easy to bear at first, saying to myself, oh, of course, I'd explain and pay you back and you wouldn't mind. But when I began to feel tender toward Ned I realized that it was the object from Piers you'd want, not the money. I've never been tender before, it's always been rather a rough game with me."

"As for the bronze, I am sorry about that," I said; I couldn't say anything else. "But for the money, forget it."

"Better not be forgiving," said Catherine.

"I'm not being forgiving. I don't think I do forgive you. Not yet, anyway, perhaps never."

We eyed each other. Catherine drew in a long breath. "Well, I feel better about that," she said. "I couldn't bear you to be saintly and forgive me. We'll come to some arrangement for living, shall we? I could stomach that much more easily."

"I thought you might." I was still treading warily. "We

can have an annual recrimination, if you like, date by arrangement . . . and I am sorry about Ned." I thought I knew all about broken hearts.

"Oh, he's buggered off," she said more cheerfully. "Maybe I'll get a second chance."

"Maybe." I didn't believe in second chances.

"Perhaps I can buy back the bronze," she suggested, taking hope.

"Perhaps." I was skeptical here also. "But don't try. Let the past bury itself."

"Ah, if it will," said Catherine.

I finished the coffee and selected a fig, peeling the skin back and smelling the pungent flesh. I had one mystery solved then: it was Catherine who had sold the bronze at Mallards, and in naming the vendor as Miss C. Warwick, even in confusing our voices, Barbara New had been right.

"Have you spoken of this to anyone else?" I asked Catherine. It was one way of asking your sister if she'd arranged a murder.

"No, only you and Ned. That was enough." She gave a small shudder. "Do you want a public confession?"

No, I could never think that Catherine had killed Barbara New. Besides, there had been nothing in any of her words to me on the telephone to imply that it was C. Warwick that Barbara New had expected to meet in Brayford. Rather the reverse: the identity of the C. Warwick who had sold the bronze and received the check had been as much a mystery to Barbara New as it had been to me.

But the person she had met had killed her. I was sure of it. Piers first, and then Barbara New.

I wanted Catherine to stay, but having purged herself, she insisted on driving away, leaving me sitting with the remains of the coffee, the honey from Hymettus, and the figs.

After a while I tried to stop thinking about what Catherine had told me and went upstairs to the old astronomer's tower room and got down to work again. My heart wasn't really in it, though, and other thoughts kept breaking in. The truth was that I was not finding my ancestor's collection as interesting as I had hoped. Presumably he *had* had some interesting old equipment, but it was all gone now. Maddeningly, I had discovered in his papers mention of a rare pair of small terrestrial and celestial globes made by the celebrated Mr. Jones of Holborn in the early eighteenth century. I knew from the records that they had been set in stands of bronze and walnut and their height had been about three feet and their diameter a neat fifteen inches. Beautiful and elegant objects they must have been, but alas, long since disappeared.

When the telephone rang I went to it slowly, reluctant to talk to anyone.

Before I had time to say anything, I heard Kit Temple's voice: "Christabel?"

I didn't answer, but it didn't matter, because he went on anyway. "Christabel, are you there? Are you all right? I'm sorry about last night. In fact, I'm sorry about a lot of things. Christabel, I want to see you. Christabel, answer, will you? There's something I have to tell you."

He was still talking as I slowly replaced the receiver. I kept my hand on the instrument, pressing it down as if by so doing I could somehow bottle up Kit Temple and silence him. Then slowly I softened the pressure.

My hand was still on the telephone when it rang again.

I picked it up quickly, angrily, thinking it was Kit calling once more. "Hello," I said savagely.

A friendly, matter-of-fact voice this time. "You've been quiet a long time, Christabel. Given up watching?"

"Hector!" It was my fellow amateur. "I haven't been forgetting about the stars, far from it. And by all accounts, they haven't been forgetting me either. In fact, I've got caught up with a bunch of astrologers here. Did that ever happen to you?"

"More than once. If people know you're interested in the stars in one way, they do tend to think you ought to be interested in another." He sounded immensely tolerant. "What with quasars, which are apparently immensely powerful suns receding from us at about the speed of light, and black holes, which are not holes at all, and pulsars, which are neutron stars and possibly invisible, there are so many strange objects scattered about the heavens that I *do* sometimes wonder if there may not be some we cannot yet see or detect which could influence us profoundly."

"You're alarming me." Without meaning to, he had conjured up a picture of dark bodies moving on unseen paths through the skies, sending powerful signals to which we responded without realizing it.

"Could be," he said. "How's the comet down in the decadent south?"

"Big: huge, in fact, a great ball."

"Well, soon it'll be moving away. I wonder what it will take with it? Something's bound to go. Don't you feel it? Tension, heat?"

"Heat, certainly," I said.

"Bound to affect people. Interesting, I call it." He managed to sound concerned yet detached at the same time: a marvelous temperament. I couldn't match it.

I was glad when he went on to ask me the technical question he had telephoned to ask; I answered it and put the receiver down. But this time I was careful to leave it off the hook.

I went to the window and looked out. From here I could see Axwater, the slope above it, and the edge of the woods. I thought I could see someone standing there looking up at me.

I ran down the winding staircase and out the door, and stood looking toward the woods where the figure had been.

Now there was no one at all.

At once the feeling that I was being watched, which had gone away during Catherine's dramatic visit, came back in strength.

Slowly I went down the steps and along the path to the lake, walking toward the spot in the woods where I had seen the figure. Had it been a man or a woman? I wasn't sure.

I came up to the gap between two trees where I thought the watcher had stood. "Hello?" I called. "Anyone here?"

Silence answered me except for the lazy humming of a bee. A dark-blue butterfly fluttered slowly in front of me and settled on a leaf, poised for a moment between flights.

"Hello?" I said again, not expecting an answer; nor did one come. Nothing was to be heard except the heavy hum of the bees. There must have been a wild colony somewhere close at hand.

I walked farther into the woods. The faint path through shrubs and trees was very narrow, better suited to animals than humans. I followed it cautiously, wondering all the time if someone was there, just beyond my vision. It was oppressively hot under the trees.

I followed the path, brushing creepers and waving ten-

196

drils away from my face as I did so. The woods covered no large area, but to me they had always seemed limitless. Even so, I was unsurprised when a turn in the path brought me out of the tangle of bushes and trees, and into the clearing where Piers and I used to meet.

Unerringly, unguided, my feet had brought me here. Just opposite me was our tree, our letter box.

I looked once, and looked again. For a minute my brain failed to comprehend what my eyes had taken in.

Around the hole in the tree trunk someone had arranged—composed might be a better word—a little wreath of plaited leaves and flowers. I went and looked. It was charmingly done. It looked the sort of decoration a Botticelli wood nymph might have worn, and it was also perfectly fresh, with not a drooping leaf or dying petal.

As if inspired, I put my hand into the hole and felt around. There was a folded piece of paper inside, which I drew out. I unfolded it: the writing on it had a thin, brown look, as if it had weathered a thousand years.

I read: "I waited and you did not come. So I will come to you."

There was no signature. But none was needed. A trembling started near my hand and spread rapidly all over my body. A letter from Piers: but how could that be?

I started to run blindly through the woods, heading for the sanctuary of the old observatory.

It seemed a long way back, with my heart thudding, and all the time the feeling that someone was watching me. There was a long scratch across my arm where a bramble had torn it, and my face was sweating when I got back. I was afraid. Afraid of what?

Afraid of who was coming: it was as simple as that.

Inside the observatory I tried frantically to get in touch with someone: Catherine, Simon, Grace May, even Kit Temple.

Catherine was not yet back home; Grace May was out, so Dr. Montague said; and Kit Temple was not answering his phone.

Eventually I got through to Simon. "Oh darling Christabel," he said at once. "I knew you'd ring."

I broke in. "It's Piers—I've had another letter."

There was a moment of silence, then he said in a clipped voice, "Piers is dead. Dead. He's dead, Christabel." I could tell he was intensely angry. With me, I supposed. Surely not with Piers?

"He's coming to see me."

"Control yourself. You're getting hysterical."

The sharpness steadied me, and I took a deep breath before speaking again. "No, Simon. I'm calm now and I *have* had a letter. Well, a note really. A few scribbled words. He's coming to see me." He didn't say anything. "Simon?"

"Be quiet; I'm thinking." Then he said, still in that cold, crisp way, "Do nothing."

"That's hard." I desperately wanted to do something.

"Do nothing," he repeated, "then meet me at Brayford station tomorrow early. We'll go right away."

"I can't run away."

"It's often a very good thing to do."

"I can't run away from Piers."

"Piers, Piers, he's all you think of. You're mad. You don't know what you're saying."

"I only know I must stay and wait for whoever or whatever comes to see me. I'll wait for twenty-four hours. If no one has come by then, I will go to the police and tell them everything."

"Oh, Christabel!" He sounded despairing. "Be reasonable. I'm pleading with you."

"I've got the letter," I said. "I'll show them the letter."

"Are you sure about that letter, Christabel? I mean,

well, I don't want to cast doubts or anything, but it *is* strange. You're not . . ." he hesitated, "imagining anything?"

"No!" I was indignant.

"It's what they'll think. That, or that you wrote it yourself. You didn't, did you?"

The gulf between us had opened wider than I could ever have thought possible. How could he think me the sort of girl he plainly did think me? Imaginative, hysterical and dishonest? "No, I didn't write it, Simon," I said, with what dignity I could. And I wondered at the quality of the love he offered me, when it seemed so strangely compounded of skepticism and distrust. But it was the same with Kit. What kind of a world of love had I fallen into? Perhaps the fault was mine.

I sat still for a few minutes, then I went over to the table where I had put the letter, and looked at it.

There was nothing on it at all. No message, no writing. Just a blank sheet of paper in the sunlight.

The day seemed to get hotter and hotter, the sky changing color subtly until the hard, deep blue was tinged with a coppery turquoise. The comet was flamboyant in this sky, its tails streaming in the solar wind—which is no wind at all, but radiation.

I was conscious of all this; it sharpened my mood. I knew that this was a strange day on which anything might happen.

I moved restlessly about the observatory, upstairs and down, listening and waiting. Would Piers come? And if he came, in what shape and manner would he come? I waited for him, dead or alive.

For the very first time I put that thought into words: was I waiting for a living, breathing Piers, or a revenant?

Or had I imagined it all, as Simon had suggested to me?

Had there been no letter, no message, nothing except a fantasy born out of my own unhappy spirit? Was it I that haunted the old observatory with my imaginings? Christabel Warwick and no one else?

And yet the physical image of the written message remained with me so clearly that I could not believe it had not existed as a real thing. Perhaps if I looked at the paper I would see it was there? But no, it wasn't.

I went into the kitchen to make some coffee, and while the water was heating I made and ate a sandwich. I sat down at the table to drink the coffee. After that I felt more rational, not at all the sort of girl who believed in ghosts. Still I wished I had someone with me, even a cat or a dog would have done.

My thoughts made a prompt switch to the cage I had seen in Folly House. Could I believe that Piers had been kept shut up in it? It was a nasty picture; it couldn't be real. The cage had been real enough, though, and the box of Piers's possessions had been real too, as had the blow on my head and my own imprisonment in the room.

Solid, actual facts in my hand, I told myself, and I opened and shut my right hand as if I held them in it.

All through the rest of that long day I waited inside the old observatory for Piers to come. My hearing became sensitized so that I heard every creak and contraction of the old building, and each one seemed to announce his arrival.

The feeling of someone being there, of my being watched, had quite gone now, and was replaced by a strong sense of expectancy. It was like waiting for a train to come in, a train that was going to sweep me off on a journey half longed for, and half dreaded.

Excitement and fear jostled for first place in my mind. As it got darker, fear edged ever so slightly forward.

"All right," I said aloud. "So, I'm frightened. It's a perfectly normal reaction to the unknown."

A door banged downstairs and I stood up, listening. There was no further sound, so slowly and with some apprehension I went down the staircase.

Nothing was there, but the front door was banging in the slight wind that had risen with evening. Had I left the door open myself? Yes, I must have done so, in an unconscious effort to make Piers's arrival easier.

It didn't occur to me then (although it did later) that I was all the time making excuses for the odd events that were building up round me, trying to take the responsibility for them on my own shoulders.

I was still standing there when I heard a little, soft panting noise. I looked down and there at my feet was a small white dog. I recognized one of the Pekes from Folly House, but I could not have said which one; they all looked the same to me although Kit Temple appeared to distinguish them.

I wondered if he had sent it to me, but Pekes aren't like sheepdogs or St. Bernards, you don't send them anywhere as messengers, for the simple reason that they would not go.

"Hello, dog," I said.

I bent down and patted the dog's head and ran my hand over his body. His flanks were heaving as if he'd been running.

I picked him up and took him in to the kitchen and offered him a bowl of water; he drank thirstily. I was puzzled, but not yet alarmed. And at least I now had company.

Night had come and I went around turning on lamps. I wanted the whole tower blazing with lights, whether in welcome or in warning, I was not yet clear.

I unfolded the sheet of paper and looked at it again.

This time the light from a table lamp struck it at an angle and I could see faint shadows on the paper. I lifted it up and held it against the light: the sentence was visible, like a watermark.

"I waited and you did not come. So I will come to you."

I put the paper down, sure now of my own rationality, but deeply puzzled. The letter had been written in ink that had bleached in the sunlight. Secret writing, you might call it.

Secret writing from a secret lover?

In spite of the lamps there were dark corners everywhere in the observatory, and there was a lot of darkness inside me too. I sat there, hugging the dog and waiting for someone who, if he came, I would hardly know.

How would he come? Would I hear feet on the stairs, a tap at the door? Or would he suddenly be there in the room with me?

Then the dog growled: one long, rumbling growl, and he stood up on my lap.

Someone had entered the tower.

I went to the curve of the stairway and called: "Who's there?"

I heard the door close.

"Who's that at the door?"

It was like a fairy story. "Who's that coming through my door?"

Slowly I went down the staircase, clutching the dog. I was grateful for his warm, muscular body pressed against me.

At the turn of the stair, I paused. A figure was silhouetted against the moonlight.

"Piers?" I said. "Piers, is that you?"

The figure came toward me. "Don't go on calling him; he would have come by now if he could."

It was a woman's voice, light yet severe: Grace May's.

"I wasn't calling," I said. The dog growled quietly.

"Yes, you were, you have been calling all the summer," she said sadly. "I've heard you, if no one else has. Oh, don't worry, child. It's only another name for grief. But have done with it now and bury him."

"I had a letter from him. Or it purported to be from him," I said. "It is difficult to bury someone who writes you letters."

"Such as Piers is now do not write letters. Oh, he may communicate, if he chooses. I do believe it is in his power to do so, if he wishes. Such has always been my belief. But letters, no."

"Someone wrote," I said, watching her. Her eyes were bright and fevered. I wondered if she was mad.

"Revenge wrote, hate wrote, stupidity wrote," she said.

She *was* mad, I thought.

"They were meant to alarm, and they *did* alarm," she said.

"*You* wrote those letters to me. That was cruel, cruel." As she had read my mind, so I read hers now.

"I wasn't thinking of you. To me you were nothing but an instrument."

"I don't understand you." I edged away from her, trying to retreat.

"Do you know that old poem about the schoolmistress who murdered her favorite pupil? Britten turned it into a song. Little Sir William, it's called. A sad song. I killed *my* favorite pupil, I see that now."

"Are you telling me that you killed Piers?"

She wasn't really seeing me at all, but looking into a world of her own. "Of all my pupils he was my brightest and best."

"Did you murder him?" I was almost shouting. But I got through to her, she seemed to see me again.

She took a deep breath. "No, no. Not with my own

203

hands. But I helped set up the conditions for it. And so did you."

"Oh, *that* sort of talk," I said bitterly. I wanted the real killer, the one with actual hands. "And don't talk about me, I loved him."

"And were loved. And he was killed because he loved. Oh yes, haven't you seen that? Jealousy is the key. Money, too. Possessions certainly were a motive."

How much more she seemed to know about it all than I had guessed. Suddenly she didn't seem dangerous any more, nor mad; she shrank to a grief-stained little old woman.

"I want to talk to you," I said gently. "Come upstairs and I'll give you some coffee. And since you came here tonight, I guess you want to talk to me."

"You're in danger," she said. "That's why I labored up here. I don't think I am myself, although I ought to be."

"No ought about it." I felt gentle toward her now, and also relieved. How strange to say that, but it was so. Piers was dead. I did not need to fear his ghost.

I poured her some coffee. The night seemed to be getting hotter, if anything. Every so often there was a distant rumble of thunder.

"Why did you send the letters?" I asked.

"From the very beginning all of us, a little group of us here in Steeple Minden, felt that there was something wrong about Piers's death. I'm not surprised you got to hear about it. But it was so hard to break through to the person who had arranged it. I suspected, oh yes, but to prove, even to get a reaction from him, that was another thing. So when you came back and were looking for him, I thought that if I wrote, as from Piers, the murderer would be alarmed and would show it. And he did, he did, I saw guilt in his face. So I tried once more, with the second letter written in saffron juice and rue, but I didn't realize how close I was to toppling him. Already he has killed two people, Piers and that poor woman in the car."

"I brought her in," I said. "That was my fault."

"I wanted so much to alert you, to tell you obliquely as much as I could." She touched my hand, trying to find reassurance from me. "But you must never think I do not believe in the cards or the planchette, for I have often found them very true as guides. I emphasized always that they were only guides." She sounded very shaky.

"Yes, you did." Gently I withdrew my hand. "And that evening you all came here, had you and Alba Bailey fixed up some little arrangement to make sure you summoned a spirit? I thought I detected something."

"Alba was to help me." She looked down at the table. "I told her I wanted to get through to Piers, that Piers would speak and she was to say she saw him, but—" and she raised her head and looked at me directly "—the boy called out before we could do anything. Whatever he saw, whatever any of us saw then, was beyond my powers."

But not beyond your powers of suggestion to anyone else, I thought, beginning to be irritated again.

"The doctor didn't like me doing any of it."

"Oh, he knew?"

"Oh yes, he knew." She sounded wretched.

"I heard him say to you, 'Don't push her.' What did he mean?"

"He thought I was building up too much pressure on you with what he called my 'tricks.' 'Mental bullying,' he called it. But I felt I had to do it." She wrung her hands. "Oh—I ought to have said outright, told you what I thought, but he's so plausible. I could see he'd make you fond of him. Love him even."

She seemed to think I knew who she was talking about, and I thought I did. Distantly I could hear Kit Temple saying, "Old Mother May, the old witch, doesn't care for me, you know. We've clashed and I've won."

A flash of lightning, followed by a roll of thunder, penetrated the room, and the lights dimmed. Rain was pelting down outside. She gave a cry and knocked over the coffee.

"It's only the storm," I said.

"No, it's not that, someone's just come into the house. Can't you hear?"

I could hear nothing, but as if to support her, the dog growled.

"I'm sure there's someone." She stood up. "I'm going to look."

"I wish you wouldn't." But I watched as she ran to the head of the stairs and peered down.

She took one step down, head craning forward as if to see, as if she could *see* something. Then a strange little cry came from her, half of fear, half (or so it seemed) of recognition.

Then, before my horrified eyes, she slumped to the floor.

"Who's come, who has?" I asked, but it was useless. She was unconscious.

I put my hand on her breast and felt her fluttering heart: she had had some sort of heart seizure. I knew I had to get help. She looked to me as if she might die without it.

And I still did not know who was in the house.

The nearest telephone was in an alcove in the turn of the stairwell. I went toward it. I tried to look only toward the telephone and not down the stairs. Inevitably, however, I was impelled to look. Nothing was to be seen: Only the empty stairs leading to the small hall.

I tried the phone, but it was dead. The storm, I supposed.

I walked down the stairs to the door. At the bottom I glanced toward the downstairs rooms which I had given over to Simon, where light from the staircase penetrated without illuminating.

In one corner stood a figure, face averted, head down, quite still. I could make out the outline of the quilted, hooded gown that had been worn by my ancestor, the old astronomer.

I knew now who had come back.

But I had better eyesight than Grace May and was not in such an emotional state, although God knows emotional enough. I didn't confuse him with any ghost.

"Take that off." My voice shook. "You look monstrous in it."

He came forward very, very slowly, not saying anything. So, of course, I had to keep talking.

"Why are you wearing it?"

He was close, I could see his face.

"I wanted to frighten you."

"But that's sick." I was sure he meant to kill me anyway, so why add an extra dimension of terror?

He explained: "To frighten you *more*."

"I'm not frightened." Grace May had been frightened, frightened to death.

"Oh yes, you are; I can tell. Inside you, you're shaking."

"I thought you loved me."

"I wanted you. I still do." He smiled, Death viewing the feast.

"Oh, Simon."

"But I can want you in pain and humiliation even more."

I shuddered. "There's a name for that," I said.

"Oh yes, and I'm it. I'm definitely it." He came forward, throwing the hood back onto his shoulders. It was the same face, with the same half-dreamy expression. I felt baffled and almost disappointed: people ought to change when you know them as they really are.

"I could have loved you decently once," he went on. "But it was Piers. He always had everything first and best. Even at nursery school, it was always he who won everything. When he met you I used to watch you together and imagine that I was with you and not him. I wanted to take his place."

"But that is not why you killed him," I said. "You killed him because he discovered you had been stealing valuable old objects, in particular one of his uncle's Chinese jars, and selling them."

"To make dreams come true you need both abilities and money," observed Simon. "I knew how much I needed to go to the high mountains, and this place was littered with antique scientific instruments that no one either cared about or knew the value of. It was easy."

"I knew," I said. "And I have been gradually coming to the truth as I worked here. I would have suspected you, even if Piers had not guessed that it was you who stole his uncle's property."

"I overreached myself there," admitted Simon. "But I was in there one day with Piers and it was so easy to go back later . . . ah well, when all was said and done, it was Piers who died, not me." He smiled slightly, still very confident of himself. "It was a pity he found out and threatened to tell his uncle. . . . I asked him to meet me one morning, he was to pick me up, I said I'd go with him to see his uncle, me making a clean breast of it. . . . I got there first, he didn't expect me, I got my hands on his throat—there's a point where pressure brings instant unconsciousness, not strangling. Just one small bruise and a broken bone. You can even do it with a quick blow like this." He showed me the edge of his hand with fingers extended. "I used it with her."

"Barbara New? You were hidden in the car beside her, no wonder her face looked distorted." Suddenly I could see the picture, the two of them in the car, the woman driving in terror.

"Yes. I had a knife. At the right spot, I stopped her by threatening her with the knife, then struck her on the throat and set the car off on a crash course. Much the same technique as with Piers. They both let me come close because they trusted me. Barbara New was a bit in love with me; I encouraged that. It was a pity she had to get a conscience and start to worry."

He sounded petulant. "I didn't want to kill her. I swear that when I met her in the town and got in her car to ride with her, all I meant to do was to—calm her down. Get her to go back to London without seeing you, if I could. I didn't want to kill her. I mean, I'm not a killer."

He looked at me as if he expected me to agree. "No," I said, carefully keeping my tone neutral.

"I liked the woman, I really did. And she loved me, women nearly always like me, and I thought that would keep her quiet. But she started talking about integrity." His mouth gave a sour twist. "Well, I did what had to be done. My hands seemed to move spontaneously. My body's always thought more quickly than my mind."

For a moment, though, his face looked haggard, and I knew that although he had used the word "technique" the two killings had not been easy for him. He was not a born killer. A feeling of hope for myself surfaced.

Instinct told me to keep still and to be quiet, to be as neutral as possible without being either docile or submissive. Too much swing of the emotional pendulum would arouse him. Keep him talking and calm him down, that was the classic advice, was it not?

But he turned on the emotion himself. "I disliked killing *her*. It was the terrible coincidence of that bronze statue of Piers's turning up for sale at Mallards, and then your telephone call."

"My sister sent it," I said. "I know all about the sale. What I don't know is why you sent the statuette to me." I picked up the little dog and held him to me protectively. All this time I had been conscious that he was keeping up a low growling. Simon had noticed it, too. I saw him looking.

He shrugged. "Superstition, I suppose. Piers had wanted you to have it, and I felt nervous about keeping it. I destroyed his will because it mentioned me. But I sent you his legacy—thus, by one of those nice little ironies, ensuring my undoing, and yours. I bet Piers is up there laughing." I moved uneasily. "Well," Simon said, "he won't laugh long."

"I have to get a doctor for Grace May," I said. "She's ill." I suppose I thought to take his mind off me.

"Oh yes?" He smiled. "You're still frightened, aren't you? Nervous as a kitten. Of me. I like that. All that business about the letters: did you write them yourself?"

"Don't be silly," I said sharply.

"No? So it was Grace May? I know her Machiavellian mind. You don't answer." He nodded. "So I'm right. Only it doesn't matter. You should have come away with me, Christabel, when I asked. I pleaded, didn't I? But no, you had to know best: off to see Kit Temple and off to the police, that was what you said." He shook his head. "I've hit you once, so I can certainly do so again. I followed you into Folly House yesterday and waited for you upstairs. I've always wanted to know where Piers's diary was and what it said. Thanks to you, I found it. By the way, *I* have the keys," and he patted his pocket and smiled. "But you'll never see the diary."

I put the dog down and edged toward the door, preparing to open it and run. But he saw me and stretched out an arm that barred my way.

"You look very attractive when you are like this, Christabel. Your eyes are quite enormous." He dragged off the quilted robe and let it fall to the floor; a strange, musty, smoky smell arose from the old silk. "But you always attract me in this place. There's a good deal of sex in the atmosphere, have you noticed?"

I began to think he was mad, or drunk, or high on drugs of some sort.

"No, I'm not imagining it, so don't screw your eyes up and raise your eyebrows in that cool little way you have, my icy girl. The old astronomer built his tower on an ancient temple site: Bronze Age or earlier. That's how Piers came by your little bronze statue. He found it here. It was a votive offering, a fertility symbol probably. Axwater is full of them. There's a phallic symbol in the tower itself, the lead object. And that's not so old, either." He gave a laugh. If my eyes were bright, his were brighter. But he wasn't mad, he was whipping himself along with the force of his own emotions. "Oh yes, this is a cult place, dedicated to the rites of love." He stretched his arms out wide, fingers extended. "And you can feel it in every inch of you."

His fingers touched mine. They were burning hot.

"How cold you are," he said. "Like death, that's what they say, isn't it?"

"Prematurely, in my case."

"A little anticipatory chill."

"No." I could hardly get the word out—he had grasped my wrist, drawn me toward him, and put one arm round me; I was pressed against him. "No," I said again as he put his lips on mine and kissed me hard.

211

"Anticipating again," he said softly, a whispered breath in my ear. "I intend to do a lot more than that."

I wrenched my head round. "Simon, how could you be like this? I really liked you."

From upstairs I heard a voice calling weakly, "Christabel, Christabel, are you there?"

Simon clapped a hand over my mouth. "Don't answer. Let her lie there."

I tried to drag myself away from him. The dog was scuffling round our feet, snapping indiscriminately at both of us. I wanted to get out the door: then I would make for the woods.

Simon kept his hand over my mouth. "I can almost read what's in your mind in your eloquent eyes. Escape. But where can you go? Into the woods? To Kit Temple?" Still holding on to me, he wrenched the door open. "Look. Look out there."

I stared: the night sky was very dark, the stars like bright holes punctured in it. Moving through the sky, riding the clouds, was the comet in all its sinister beauty.

But beyond Axwater, in the direction of Folly House, the sky had a different light. I could smell smoke.

"The woods are burning. Folly House is alight. I've shot Kit Temple in the leg, and with one of his own guns; he's lying there with house and woods burning around him. I did it." Simon's voice was rising with his excitement, he was dragging me out of the house, onto the top of the steps. "Everything is going to burn, it will all go up in smoke and flame. It is the end of everything, like the burning of Valhalla, the Götterdämmerung: the death of the gods."

He had his arm tightly round me, gripping me hard. I could feel a trickle of blood from my lower lip where he had kissed me. He pressed his face against mine again and I gave a small involuntary scream and pushed him away.

212

At the same moment, the dog leapt for him. I saw his jaws fasten on Simon's hand. Simon gave a shout. He was momentarily off balance: I shoved; he fell backward, with the dog still hanging on to him, and I was off and away. Running, running toward Folly House.

I could hear him stumbling behind, shouting, and all the time the dog was barking. Ahead lay water, and behind, on the rising ground, the woods sheltering Folly House. It was these, tinder-dry, that were burning. As the fire spread, people would see it, help would come, I would be rescued.

But I couldn't wait. Simon wasn't going to wait. When he kissed me he had done so without love, even without passion—which I could have accepted and even acquiesced in—but as if he was anxious to impress himself upon me, to wipe me out. He wanted to work me over with hobnailed boots, and this was his way of doing it. At the end of it I would be dead and dumped in the lake. Or thrown into the woods to burn.

I didn't feel like being a victim, and as I ran I was thinking. So many events had been thrown at me in this last hour that I had not yet got sorted out: as well as my own personal crisis, there was Grace May, lying desperately ill, and above and beyond all there was Kit, who might already be dead. Shock, which should have bewildered me, had instead suspended time. The minutes were passing very, very slowly. My run toward the lake seemed already to have been going on forever, and my limbs seemed to move in slow motion. But my brain was crystal clear and I was strangely calm. Axwater still seemed a long, long way to run, but as I got closer I saw that I was not the only soul to seek refuge there. The lake was ringed with animals. Large beasts and small had crept down to the water to find safety from the flames.

Some were actually up to their hocks in the water; others crowded in the rushes and grasses. Ancient enmities were forgotten: a fox stood immobile beside a pair of rabbits; a deer, large-eyed and nervous, let a squirrel sit between its legs; a badger watched me with beady eyes. A group of Kit Temple's special White Park cattle stood together as if for mutual protection.

They looked formidable, gentle but strong beasts. Without a look behind me, I slid into the water where they stood, and hid myself among them.

Simon was splashing through the water looking for me. He was shouting my name. I kept quiet and still, praying that the animals would not move. They shuffled uneasily, moving their feet, but they stayed together. I crouched there, glad of the lull. Time had gone back to working at its normal speed.

The fire was spreading rapidly. Every so often a little flight of sparks trailed across my field of vision, making a weird parallel with the stars in the sky and the lion-tailed comet. Once or twice I saw the flash of lightning.

Then I realized that for some minutes I had heard nothing from Simon or the dog. I stood cautiously: he had crept round Axwater and come upon me from behind. He was standing there looking at me.

Silently we regarded each other. Then he mouthed something at me. He didn't have to tell me what it was: I knew. He was going to kill, and degrade me first, if he could.

I moved backward, retreating into the water. I was facing the burning trees; Simon had his back to them. Also, he was obsessively focused on me.

So I saw what he did not: a machine was moving out of the woods, slowly and cautiously feeling its way through. No headlights were on, but suddenly I recognized it as the Folly House Range-Rover.

Kit must be alive.

Even as I looked, I saw the Range-Rover edge slowly forward, and I could actually make out Kit's figure. A few more yards and he stopped the vehicle. I saw he had a gun. And he had seen me. I knew it.

A great feeling of happiness and renewed hope flowed through me. I suppose it must have been reflected in my expression, and provided the last touch of the lash that Simon needed. He jumped into the shallow water and moved forward swiftly, reaching out for my throat. But my skin was wet, his hands slipped, and I wrenched myself away to drag myself up the muddy slope from the lake. He caught hold of my skirt, but I struggled forward. I wrenched my skirt free.

A voice called: it was Kit. "Don't move, Christabel. Stay where you are. I'm going to shoot."

Just as he said it I knew I didn't want him to shoot Simon, not even at the cost of my own life. It was love for Kit, not pity, that moved me. I wanted to be with Kit forever. I knew that instinctively now, and I thought yet another death would separate us forever. Simon and Piers would stand between us, united in death as they had not been in life.

I kicked, and the force of my kick sent Simon reeling, falling backward among the cattle at the water's edge. I heard the animals make a frightened noise. At that moment there was a tremendous flash of lightning, followed by a loud roll of thunder. As I turned to look, I saw the terrified beasts rearing and stamping, and Simon underneath their hooves. I heard him scream. His head seemed to disappear into the mud. There was blood on the water.

When Kit, with difficulty because of his wounded leg, got himself down the slope to me, I was face-down on the turf, weeping. I swear I do not know for whom.

Kit came and sat beside me and put his hand on my shoulder. For some moments we sat without talking. I have told Kit of how Simon talked to me in the tower, of his confession, and of the nature of his threats to me. But although we have been married for over a year, we have never spoken of those last minutes of Simon's life. Until now, when the time seems right.

I understand him so much better now, and appreciate both his strength and his sensitivity; I know what caused his extraordinary withdrawal from the world. They have great powers of haunting themselves, this family, the Temples. I had seen it in Piers: haunted by suffering, he had chosen to become a doctor. Kit blamed himself for the death of his own brother, Piers's father. The family inheritance had been divided equally between them, but whereas Kit had kept his, and even managed to increase it, Piers's father had gambled away his share. Money had been part of the family crisis that had sent him abroad and parted Piers and me in the first place. Then had come a fatal car crash in Kit's own car. "I half believed he crashed on purpose," Kit had said to me, "and half believed it was my fault. I'd refused to lend him any more money, you see. And it was I who had taught him the fun of gambling in the first place—although for me it was never more than amusement. I was luckier, too. Then when Piers died so terribly, and just when we had quarreled, I felt as if I had wiped out my entire family. I had to hide. I *did* hide. And then I thought, No, you've got to come back into the world. That's why I took up mathematics: to stretch my mind, to make sure of the forces of reason. I've always felt there was a pretty big bag of unreason inside me, as there is in all of us, God knows."

Yes, I understand him so well, and understand how to talk to him and to tell him, at last, about Simon. Even to
216

admit that I had, for a little while, been attracted. Between us two all things can be spoken now.

He took a restless turn up and down the room (we were in the newly redecorated library at Folly House) before answering. As always, the three dogs watched him, beady-eyed. "I suppose I always knew it," he said. "He really was sick, wasn't he?"

I nodded.

"Just shows how important childhood is. We'll have to remember that."

I nodded again.

"Glad you didn't tell me that night. I don't know what I'd have done. Except he was dead already."

"And you were lame," I pointed out. Kit still limped; his left knee would never be quite repaired.

"Yes: he nearly did it for me. I had no idea he was in the house that night. Of course he had your keys. But I wasn't thinking of him. I was still thinking of the police who had visited me, saying they were opening up an inquiry into the death of Miss New and the sale of my Chinese jar. I understood that Piers had not stolen my jar then, and a shadow lifted. It freed me."

"And you were upset about our quarrel," I said; I could talk about that now too. "I've forgiven you for thinking I was an hysterical lunatic the night Simon hit me on the head and took off with Piers's diary. I suppose if I'd read it, a lot would have been made clear to me."

"Well, we will never know." The diary had never been found. All through the restoration of the burned part of the house, I had been wondering if it would turn up. But it never had. "It doesn't worry you, does it, darling?"

"Not in the least." I felt very calm, placid even. No doubt it was a temporary state, but it was enjoyable while it lasted. Still, tranquil and secure as I was, I did not tell Kit that I had once suspected him of having kept

Piers as a prisoner in a cage. Even the most phlegmatic of husbands (and Kit is not that) might resent the idea. I think I was a little mad myself that night. The cage, as I knew now, had held a sick deer, temporarily cared for there by old Joss.

"Pregnancy suits you." He smiled at me. "Boy or girl? Make any difference?"

"Grace May says she has seen it in the stars: first a girl and then a boy," I observed. "These days she's consulting the stars."

Grace May had recovered, although she was still something of an invalid. She had put aside the Tarot pack, and no longer referred to Kit as either The Hermit or The Magician. There was an enigmatic look in her eyes, though, when she spoke of him, so I guessed the old Grace lived yet.

"And what do *your* stars say?" He took my hand.

"Well now, let me see," I said thoughtfully. "As you know, I've been down to the observatory almost every day. It's in splendid order now, by the way, and that new telescope that you . . ."

"Not those stars—your own particular private, personal ones, those are the ones I mean. What do they tell you?"

For a moment I was back in the immediate past.

The cards had had one last game to play with me before they were done. About a month after the violent events at the old observatory, and when Grace May had recovered sufficiently to be able to see visitors, I was invited to her house. Summoned, really, it was, as usual: Grace was not so greatly changed.

The invitation was conveyed by Dr. Montague. "I'll take you down there under my wing," he announced cheerfully. "Just a little gathering of friends. Just us, in fact. Tomorrow, round five o'clock."

"I'm glad Miss May is so much better."

"Not quite herself yet, but coming on nicely. Just one little job to be done, and she wants you there."

"Oh?" I said apprehensively; I had reason to be wary of Grace May.

"No need to be nervous, my dear. I'll be there."

"I'll come along. Tomorrow, then?"

"We'll go together." He patted my hand. "Grace expects us. You'll be gentle with her? I won't say she's a changed woman, nothing could change Grace, but she's been a scared woman. She's touched forces she couldn't control and she knows it."

"The Tarot cards, you mean?"

"Not just the cards, but the anger and violence in Simon. She tried to use them for her own revenge." He shook his head. "Won't do, you know, won't do. I told her that at the time."

When we got to Grace May's the next evening, I had looked round to see if Kit was there; I was already beginning to feel incomplete without him, but we were the only people in the room.

Bright golden sunlight filled the room. It was a lovely early autumn evening, cool after the heat of the summer.

Grace May was sitting on a chair placed in the window bay, but she stood up as we came in and held out her hand. She looked thinner but otherwise much as before. Only in her manner was there a softness and almost a shyness I had never seen before.

"I'm so glad you've come. I knew you would, and I want you here. There's one last thing I have to do. One final little ceremony." She spoke solemnly.

"And what's that?"

Stiffly, she walked across to the wall cupboard where she kept the Tarot cards, took them out, and set them on the table. Beside them she put a plain wooden box.

"We must put the cards to sleep."

You haven't changed so much, I thought. I said, "Is that necessary?"

"I think so." She opened the box. "For thirty years I have called up the powers that lie in the cards, and used them. The cards are now awake."

I glanced at Dr. Montague: I thought he gave me a very slight wink.

"They vibrate with life. Can't you feel?" And she put my right hand onto the cards.

To my fury, I did feel a very faint tingle in my fingers. Imagination, no doubt. I pulled my hand away smartly.

"Yes, you feel it," she said. "Now we must put the cards to sleep." She held out her hands, one to me, one to Dr. Montague. "Now, you two take hands. Form a circle. Don't move round widdershins, it's unlucky. In fact, don't move, stand still."

Whether I wanted to or not, I was compelled to take my part in the circle. In a soft voice, she said, "Let us call upon those forces inside us and outside. Let us call upon those cosmic forces that move both cards and comets, and also upon those energies within us which unite with them."

I shifted my hands. How hot and heavy they felt.

"Let us ask for rest. Rest for the cards. Sleep for the strength within them. Only sleep, not death. Sleep, Priestess; sleep, Master Magician; sleep, Fool."

I wanted to say, "Oh, what rubbish," but the sincerity in her voice and face kept me quiet.

Then she said, with satisfaction, "The cards are quiet. Emperor and Empress, Hermit and Lion, all of whom are separate beings and yet one and the same, all sleep."

I withdrew my hands. "If you say so."

"Feel." She pushed my hands down onto the Tarot pack. "Quiet, aren't they? Now pick them up."

"If I must."

"Heavy, aren't they?"

I put the pack back on the table and shrugged. Not for anything would I have admitted that the cards felt as heavy as lead. "Why did you need me?" I asked.

"Oh, my dear, because you are part and parcel of it all. I used you, and for that I will never forgive myself, but you do realize, do you not, that the energies released within you contributed as well? Perhaps you even drew the comet here. That young, restless, vital force within you was very strong. Virginity brings its own fires, my dear, and that is why the ancients feared it."

"You take a lot for granted," I said coldly.

"The cards are never wrong. Never mind. It is a burden of which you will soon be relieved."

"Really, Grace," said Dr. Montague.

"No, she wants to know." Turning back to me, she said, "The turbulence will subside. No more ghosts, Christabel. No more comets. No more fires. You will be happy."

And that was that. The Tarot cards were locked away in their box, presumably, in Grace May's eyes at least, in a state of suspended activity (for I saw she thought of it more as a hibernation than sleep), and I was free to go.

"Don't be too hard on her," said Dr. Montague, as he led me out. "I know she says outrageous things, but there's a lot of truth in them. And you will be very happy with that young man up at Folly House." To him, Kit, who was my senior by almost ten years, still seemed very young. "Your future is there, you know." He added cheerfully, "I'll tell Grace to consult the stars. She has to have something, you know."

"Tell her to come to the observatory," I said, "and consult *those* stars! I'm going to have a new telescope. Kit is going to give it to me."

The plans for Folly House had been revived. Iris's husband was going to put money into it. The restaurant was to be opened and it would specialize in English food. The beauties of the park and garden were to be restored. There was even talk of a music center with concerts in the rose garden.

Now I come back to the present and Kit's question to me.

"I don't have to look to the stars," I answered. "I know that I am happy. I know the best way: by being so."

The comet had its period of glory, then gradually left us, to come back perhaps on a distant day. There are no ghosts in the old observatory. Even the figure with "hungry" eyes that old Joss had seen walking in the woods proved to be no specter. He was Piers's old friend Little Billy, who had been so plump and was now so thin, with big dark eyes. He is a young medical student. I met him again when I was visiting Grace May in hospital. "I walked there, in the woods, hoping to meet you," he had confided shyly. "You and Piers were always so nice to me. I longed to meet you again."

Sometimes I do think I see Piers walking in the woods, but when I hurry forward it is only the leaves moving in a breeze or an animal disappearing into a thicket. Yet I feel his presence. Every day it seems to grow fainter, and I expect when the child is born even this gentle ghost will withdraw and I shall say goodbye at last to my dear young love.

Yesterday I went to the woods and whispered to the bees who carry all the news of life and death: Goodbye, Goodbye, Goodbye.

FREE
Fawcett Books Listing

There is Romance, Mystery, Suspense, and Adventure waiting for you inside the Fawcett Books Order Form. And it's yours to browse through and use to get all the books you've been wanting . . . but possibly couldn't find in your bookstore.

This easy-to-use order form is divided into categories and contains over 1500 titles by your favorite authors.

So don't delay—take advantage of this special opportunity to increase your reading pleasure.

Just send us your name and address and 35¢ (to help defray postage and handling costs).